ZANDER

by

Oliver Gray

Sarsen Press

Design: David Eno, Oliver Gray

Editorial consultant: Grace Glendinning

Published by Sarsen Press

Front cover painting by Owen Price

Back cover painting by C.S. Talley

Contact Oliver Gray at P.O. Box 71, Winchester SO21 1ZE, UK

E-mail: oliver@revilolang.com

www.olivergray.com

ISBN: 1-897609-08-8

Acknowledgements

Grateful thanks to Birgit Gray, Annabel Gray and Lucy Gray. Thanks also to David Eno and Tony Hill, plus Ian Soulsby, Attorney General's Office, The Society Of Authors (legal details), Martin Barlow (police procedure), Chris T-T, Phil Campbell and Trevor Stevens. Thank you to Jim Jones (Small Town Jones) for permission to use the lyrics from "Waves", and especially to Willy Vlautin for his encouragement and advice. Special thanks to Baz Mort for allowing his name to be purloined. Baz is not a homicidal maniac!

The settings in Winchester and Austin are authentic. The Station, The Weekly News and St John's School are fictitious, as are some of the shops and pubs. All characters are entirely fictitious apart from some music personalities listed below.

The following people all kindly gave their permission for their names to be used in the fictional context:

Chuck Prophet, Jon Dee Graham, Ian McLagan, Jon Notharthomas, Alejandro Escovedo, Chris Searles, Bobby Daniel, Peter Bruntnell, Jon Amor, James Walbourne, Amy Boone, Willy Vlautin, Sam Baker, Monte Montgomery, Bob Cheevers, Sarah Sharp, Freedy Johnson, Allan Jones.

Every effort has been made to contact everyone mentioned in the book. Apologies for any inadvertent omissions.

Finally, special thanks to the strange collection of oddballs who daily populate Eastleigh Library, where this book was written.

Chapter 1

Ben had walked the route a thousand times. Through the council estate, past the church and along the parade of shops. Every suburb had a parade like this, but because this was middle-class Winchester, it didn't contain any charity shops or betting shops and only one window was boarded up. This, sandwiched between the incongruous fireplace shop and the Indian restaurant, had been called "The Great English Takeaway". Some mad entrepreneur had come up with a concept that Dragon's Den would have annihilated. It was a take-away establishment offering delicacies such as roast beef, Yorkshire Pudding and Spotted Dick in plastic containers. Needless to say, it had only lasted weeks.

The Maharaja's Palace, next door, was lucky to be still in business. Over the previous six months, the local paper, the Hampshire Weekly News, had reported a damning inspection by health officers ("poor kitchen hygiene") plus another by the Border Agency ("employing illegal immigrants"). Cleverly, the Palace had re branded itself simply as "The Raj" ("Fine sub-continental dining"), conducted an intensive campaign on Twitter and Facebook, and was once again the area's destination of choice for a curry on a Friday and Saturday night after the pubs closed.

Ben walked past the Raj, noting, as he did every morning, that what had seemed so irresistible the night before now made him feel slightly nauseous. No wonder Indian restaurants don't open early to serve breakfast. Do you suppose, indeed, that Indians eat curry for breakfast? Ben didn't know. He marched up to the automatic doors of the Co-op, hoping they would open rather than break his nose. There was no reason to think they might not open, but that was how Ben was. You couldn't be sure they would open, any more that you could be sure of anything in life.

Opposite the parade of shops was a sign of the times. A large Waitrose had sprouted, threatening the previous quiet confidence of the street. Attached was a Costa Coffee shop, adding to the corporate blandness. The big topic of conversation in the Weekly News' letters page in recent weeks had been the application by a discount supermarket to build a branch on the site of a derelict pub adjacent to Waitrose, which itself had recently replaced a petrol station. While Waitrose (posh) had been welcomed by the locals, the discount store (cheap) had struck fear into residents' hearts. Why, it might even attract people from places like Basingstoke or – shudder – Eastleigh, in search of its appetite-satisfying delights, shipped in weekly in a container from Germany.

It was Friday, and Friday was the day the Hampshire Weekly News came out. All Ben wanted was a newspaper, but the newsagent's shop had closed soon after the arrival of Waitrose. The Co-op (whose days were also probably numbered once the discount store was up and running) sold the Weekly News. It was an anachronistically old-fashioned yet undoubtedly successful newspaper. It financed itself by including a huge property supplement each week, advertising impossibly expensive country mansions that presumably existed somewhere behind the leylandii, although Ben had certainly never seen any of them in real life. Ben bought the broadsheet and nearly injured his head on a lamp post as he shuffled along the street, leafing through its pages. Would Derek White have delivered the goods?

A decade previously, the Weekly News had employed a team of over twenty reporters and photographers. Now all that was left was an editor, a deputy editor, two writers and a photographer. Their job was to fill 48 pages with news, reviews, an entertainments guide, sports reports and everything else you'd expect from a local paper. They weren't experts on everything they wrote about, and depended largely on press releases. Sometimes, space restrictions meant that the original press release became mildly garbled. Could this have happened with the information Ben had sent them? But that was the least of his worries. The big question was whether his concert would be mentioned at all.

In four days' time, Ben would be presenting the first-ever UK gig by Corey Zander, a roots musician from Texas known only to a select audience of insiders. Ben had no money to advertise the show and had spent the last few weeks working out how to let people know about what was, after all, quite an unusual occurrence for a provincial town in the UK. It was his first attempt at being an impresario. Having often travelled to London, Oxford, Bristol and Brighton, following the music he loved, he'd been asked by the tour manager of a New York ex-punk band whether he knew of any venues suitable for Corey Zander. He didn't ... but then again, maybe he did. What about The Station?

The Station was a cheerfully run-down pub and music venue near, guess what, the train station in Winchester. It certainly didn't normally play host to troubadours from Texas, but actually, there was no reason why it shouldn't. The Station's line-up mainly consisted of tribute bands, washed-up punks, death metal outfits and, its staple diet, so-called "showcase gigs", featuring three or four local bands of youngsters who thought they were the future of rock and roll. Economic reality dictated that these were the sorts of shows that worked well in such a venue. Guitar bands were in vogue, reality TV shows had convinced parents to buy guitars for their offspring in the hope of possible instant fame, so the local colleges were bursting with four-piece bands, mainly not very good ones. But for The Station, it worked. Book four of those a night, hope they would each bring twenty of their mates, and there would be eighty youngsters buying drinks. Even if they were technically under age, the mark-up on Coke and lemonade was even better than that on beer.

Only recently, The Station had featured in the Weekly News when a bunch of under-age kids had got an older sibling to purchase mass supplies of alcohol from the local Tesco, stashed them under a bench in the pub's beer garden and proceeded to get completely wasted. The inevitable subsequent horseplay had turned into a full-scale brawl involving glass bottles and refuse from the outside dustbins being hurled around the car park. Ambulances arrived to carry away the wounded, the police made several arrests and the next morning, council officials arrived at The Station to reconsider its licence. They only relented when taking into account that the glass bottles and the alcohol within them had been bought from a supermarket and not from the pub.

When Ben had gone to The Station to enquire about how you went about booking an artist into a venue, he'd been pleasantly surprised at the reception he received. The landlord, Andy, who would probably have preferred his establishment to be a nice quiet eaterie but had been seduced by the siren sounds of the music of his youth and some ringing tills, passed Ben on to his assistant, Sam, who was in charge of the bookings. After initially looking doubtful, Sam brightened up when Ben explained that the demographic for Corey Zander was likely to be mainly middle-aged men who would doubtless be charmed by the pub's array of real ales and imbibe enthusiastically. That's what a pub likes to hear, and soon Ben had discovered that there was no mystery in putting on a show. You simply booked the venue, booked the artist, advertised the show and kept your fingers crossed.

Ben had assumed there'd be some financial outlay involved, but it wasn't too onerous. It was a hundred quid for the room and sixty to pay the sound engineer. Corey Zander's agent Glenn Wallis had asked for a guarantee of five hundred pounds plus accommodation. Corey had been banned from driving in Texas for an alcohol infringement, he explained, and wouldn't be allowed to drive in the UK. Ben did some sums and worked out the following: If fifty people attended at ten pounds a head, he'd be making quite a loss. But if sixty people came, paying £15 each, he'd more than break even. It seemed a risk worth taking to bring a semi-legend to his home town. Ben's salary as a primary teacher in a primary school in the Winchester suburbs didn't exactly make him rich, but nonetheless he decided to go for it and asked Sam to pencil a couple of dates.

This was Ben's first experience of dealing with a music agent, and it turned out to be more complicated than he'd expected. For a start, Glenn Wallis seldom replied to emails and hardly ever answered his mobile phone or returned messages. Then, when a date had finally been agreed, Ben realized for the first time, on talking to Wallis, that Corey Zander had been booked to play the night after in Basingstoke and the night after that in Southampton. Only someone severely geographically challenged could have failed to realize that these three shows would all dilute each others' audiences, being within a few miles of each other. "Really?" said the agent. "I didn't know."

The results of this dereliction of duty were already plain to see. Ben had printed out some tickets, which he was quite proud of designing himself on his laptop, but initially, there had been no one to sell them to. Record shops used to be the places to sell tickets, but Winchester hadn't had an independent record shop since Winchester Wax in Stockbridge Road had closed down a decade previously. The music shop which had taken its place refused to sell tickets or display posters on the grounds that they were busy enough as it was and had no window space. In town, there was a last remaining branch of a record store chain, doomed, no doubt, to eventual extinction by the rise of the internet and digital downloads. Their response when Ben had enquired about them selling tickets had been one of scathing scorn. "It's not our policy", was all they would say. "You could try calling Head Office." Ben's attempt to do just that had led him into a call centre chain so labyrinthine that he'd given up. He enjoyed the Schadenfreude of hoping that, before long, the place would be closed down and the staff would be made redundant.

The Station, however, did have its own method of selling tickets. An inability to choose between the baffling selection of online ticket agencies, all with their attendant "booking fees" had led to their using three of them: Ticket Web, Ticketscript and SEE tickets. The Corey Zander show was duly put on sale on all of these and Ben sat back in anticipation of advance sales, if not flooding, then maybe at least trickling in. Sam taught him how to log in and check ticket sales. This led to a ritual which started as a daily activity and eventually developed into a compulsive obsession which took place every hour or so. In the days leading up to the show, Ben discovered he could even check ticket sales on his phone, so took to having a look between every lesson. If he'd thought he could get away with it, he'd have looked during the lessons as well, but his head teacher would undoubtedly have spotted it and taken a dim view.

Four days to go, and not a single ticket had been sold.

What would be the consequences of an empty room greeting Corey Zander's first ever UK show? Well, there'd be financial fallout for sure and Ben feared grief from Rosie if she were to find out just how much he had lost. Although tolerant of Ben's love of "Americana" music (in return for which, he tolerated her addiction to Coronation Street), Rosie was of the opinion that they should both be saving for their wedding and not wasting money on self-indulgent hobbies. But she didn't know how much Ben stood to lose, and she wouldn't know. Ben would make sure of that.

As he leafed through the grandly-named "Arts" section of the Weekly News, Ben was painfully aware that this was his last chance. Like many rookie promoters in the past, he had thought that simply booking the room and the artist was enough, and hadn't budgeted for publicity. What he should have done, he realized, was taken out an ad in the local press, but when he'd enquired about advertising rates, he'd come over queasy. They were outrageous. The agent had assured him that the record company would definitely be placing ads in the "Live" sections of Uncut, Q and MOJO, plus of course, Corey's new live album would be reviewed and featured in all of them. A visit to WH Smith in the High Street the week before had allowed him to peruse all three of these publications with bated breath. He didn't buy any of them, obviously, although he might have done, for his scrapbook, if there had been any hint of the promised mentions. Ben had also dutifully sent details of the show to the listings agency which supplied the national papers with their information, but nothing had appeared in any lists.

It was obvious that Corey Zander would be entering the country with more secrecy than a Soviet spy.

Astonishingly, the record distribution company (which turned out, for reasons unknown, to be based in Belgium) had supplied Ben with twenty full-colour A3 posters, admittedly depicting a ten years younger Corey complete with a short-lived Texan backing group from whom he'd long since split acrimoniously. This was clearly the way to tell people about the gig, but what exactly was Ben to do with them? He set off round town to find places to display the posters, starting at the local Tourist Information Office. As this institution existed to promote events in the city, he was confident of a warm welcome, but the grumpy lady behind the counter could hardly contain her contempt at something which was clearly neither classical nor literary.

"I'm afraid we only have the facility to display A4 posters, so we can't help you."

"Oh, I'm sorry. What about that space over there?"

"I'm afraid that space is reserved for the Theatre Royal."

"Ah, okay, I'll see if I can get an A4 version made. Thank you."

Ben put on a display of cheerful gratefulness for even being given the time of day, but, as he negotiated another threatening set of sliding doors on exiting, he actually muttered to himself, "Thank you for nothing, mate."

Next, he went to the Council Office next door. All over the city were notice boards advertising all manner of fêtes, amateur dramatics, coffee mornings and the like. Ben wondered how to get access to these firmly locked glass-fronted cabinets, and had arranged to meet Mark Dibben, the council's "Communications Officer".

"I'm sorry", Mr Dibben explained, with a manner expressing a mixture of patronisation and intransigence, "but the event you are describing appears to be a profit-making activity and therefore doesn't meet the criteria for display on our Community Events boards."

"It certainly won't be a profit-making activity," Ben assured him. "It's just something I'm doing to provide a bit of entertainment."

"Ah, so it's a charity event?"

"Well, that's not how it was conceived, but if there's any profit, I'd be happy to donate the money to Amnesty or Greenpeace."

Mr Dibben nearly choked. "I'm afraid it would have to be a local charity."

"It looks like my only remaining option is to do a bit of fly-posting," responded Ben. "There are a few building sites around town."

"I'm afraid that if you did that, you would risk prosecution." Mr Dibben was almost glowing with the aura of a well-satisfied Jobsworth.

Odd how everyone Ben spoke to was "afraid". They bloody well soon should be afraid, he thought, as he headed back on to the High Street to seek out some shops, cafés or pubs willing to display his posters. He was rapidly coming to accept that he was more naïve than he had realized. Of course, the last thing the management of one pub wanted to do was give publicity to a rival establishment. He didn't know the derivation of the expression "short shrift", but he now knew its effect. "You've got to be kidding", was the essence of every response.

The shops in the High Street were all chains, whose managers looked blank but made it clear that putting up posters for people was not "company policy". Years ago, there had been a few independent businesses around the place, tobacconists, sweet shops and the like, with little notice boards in their windows, but Ben now realized they had all gone. Those useful A3 posters were going to have to decorate his wall at home, because there sure as hell wasn't anywhere else to put them.

There were two local, taxpayer-subsidised "Arts Centres", whose clientèle would have been the exact target audience and who doubtless held copious mailing lists, but they, of course, were unwilling to share them, citing "data protection". They wouldn't put up any posters because the event was "unofficial". Ben could have hired one of these venues, but unfortunately they were so expensive that he'd have lost even more money than it looked like he was about to lose anyway.

Ben had been sent a few Corey Zander CDs for distribution to local radio stations. Unfortunately, there weren't any – at least, any who were interested in obscure American has-beens. The BBC station, Radio

Solent, was talk-based, while the names of the two commercial stations ("Smooth" and "Wave") said all you needed to know about them. Their musical spectrum stretched all the way from Simply Red to One Direction.

That was why Derek White, the editor of the Weekly News' arts supplement, was so important, indeed crucial, and the reason for Ben to peruse the paper with such heart-thumping anticipation. Derek had promised to do a "feature" on Corey Zander in this week's paper. In order to do this, he'd explained, he would need a comprehensive biography of the performer. All Ben knew was that he was a respected "roots" artist whose music he loved, so he asked Glenn Wallis, Corey's agent, if he could fill in the background. Glenn said he'd send Ben an email with an attachment within 48 hours. After a week, Ben reminded him and he guaranteed the biography would be with him the next day. That had been a fortnight ago, so Ben had decided he'd need to research it himself. Corey Zander, unbelievably really, didn't appear to have a website, but there were plenty of references to him on the internet. His Wikipedia page was one of those minimal ones, liberally spattered with blue bits saying "unverified", but it did reveal his year of birth (1958) and his place of birth (Tahlequah, Oklahoma).

Days of web trawling had enabled Ben to create a relatively comprehensive life history of Corey Zander, and he'd found an out-of-date but nevertheless high resolution photo. He sent the lot to Derek White, who had explained that his specialities were opera and ballet, so he would need guidance.

Ben was hoping for at least half of the music page, hopefully simply printing what he'd sent in, but this morning, his last hope, was to bring bitter disappointment. A local schoolgirl called Melinda Miles had reached round two of the X-Factor and the page consisted of an inappropriately revealing photo of her, together with some quotes from her proud mother.

At the bottom of the page, there was room for two small extra paragraphs. One plugged the forthcoming appearance of a Guns 'n' Roses tribute band at a local social club. The other one was the big plug for the Corey Zander show. This is what it said:

Canadian blues star Carey Sander will be playing at Winchester's Station venue on Friday, October 14th at 7.30pm. Tickets cost £5 and are available in advance from the venue.

How could they possibly have messed this up so comprehensively? Corey was Corey, not Carey. He was Zander, not Sander. He was American, not Canadian. He wasn't really a star. He didn't play blues. The show was at 8 pm, not 7.30. October 14 was a Monday, not a Friday. Tickets were £15, not £5 and were available online or on the door only. That was going to irritate a few people turning up clutching a fiver.

It was going to be a crap day at school anyway, trying to teach with so many other things on his mind. Ben dumped the Weekly News in the litter bin outside the chippie on the corner and set off down Stockbridge Road, the rucksack full of unmarked exercise books weighing down his already slumped shoulders.

Chapter 2

Researching the history of Corey Zander had taken a lot of effort but actually been quite fun. Most of the information came from an obscure and strangely-titled fanzine called Bucketfull of Brains, which specialized in "Americana" music. Then there had been an article by Allan Jones in Uncut. Jones, having previously been the editor of Melody Maker, contributed nostalgic articles looking back at the wildest days of rock and roll. It seemed that Corey fitted neatly into that bracket. Spending a lot of time on the internet and in Winchester's library (recently re-christened, for no particular reason, as a "Discovery Centre"), Ben gradually reconstructed Corey's life.

Corey Zander, born Alexander Cruz, was the only son of Pino Cruz and his wife Aileen, delivered in their small house in Tahlequah, Oklahoma, in January 1958. Corey's great grandfather was a Choctaw Indian who had arrived in Oklahoma on the Trail Of Tears, the popular term for the forced relocation of Native American nations from the south east of the US in accordance with the Indian Removal Act of 1830. The expression "Trail Of Tears" refers to the removal of the Choctaw Nation in 1831 from their native homelands in Florida, Mississippi and North Carolina. Many of the relocated Native Americans, including Cherokee, Choctaw and Muskogee, died of starvation, exposure or disease on the cold and chaotic trail to Oklahoma. The Choctaw were the first to be removed and seventeen thousand families made the move to Oklahoma, originally called Indian Territory. Having effectively been ethnically cleansed, they eventually became known as the Choctaw Nation of Oklahoma.

By the time Pino Cruz was born in 1938, the dustbowl existence of his family had become bearable, if hard. Pino himself was able, as an adult, to earn a tolerable living as a general handyman in and around Tahlequah, while Aileen looked after young Alexander. It was when Alexander was seven that Pino was accused of stealing from one of his clients. As it happened, it was a bottle of bourbon that went missing from a house where he was repairing the roof while the owner was out. He couldn't deny it, as the bottle, now a couple of fingers lighter, was found at the bottom of his tool bag the next day, when the angry homeowner called in the police. Dissatisfied with the quality of Pino's work, and probably looking for an excuse not to pay, the owner pressed charges on what was, on the face of it, a trivial case, and Pino was fined, but what was worse, disgraced within the local community, where the word spread that anyone who employed him was likely to get burgled.

There was another unfortunate result of his foolishness, as those few slugs of deadly liquid re-awoke an interest in liquor which had long lain dormant. Financial necessity and the strong disapproval of his wife, who was frightened of the effect of whisky on Pino's temperament, had ensured many years of sobriety up to that point. It wasn't quite on the level of Shakespearian tragedy, perhaps, but that light-fingered moment represented a significant turning point in Pino's life. If he'd rationalized it, which he surely didn't, he'd have said something like "What the hell, if I work hard and a small transgression can pretty much ruin my life, what exactly is the point?" Unable to find work, and finding the stress of responsibility for a young son tough to cope with, Pino took to thieving on a regular basis, using the proceeds to fund visits of varying success to a nearby Indian Casino. When he won, he would celebrate with whiskey. To his credit, he purposely didn't drink in front of Alexander, keeping his binges until after the lad was in bed. It did mean that he was normally ill-tempered in the morning, but he wasn't the kind of drunk who'd lay his hands on his wife or son. He just felt unhappy most of the time, and the atmosphere would surely have been bad enough to encourage Aileen to leave, if she'd had the choice. But she had nowhere to go.

It would have been advantageous from the point of view of creating a myth about the upbringing of the future rock star Alexander if his father Pino had died a violent death in a car crash or a bar fight, but the reality was more mundane. In 1968, when Alexander was just 10, Pino's liver gave out and Aileen was left alone to look after the boy. By that time, the family had long since been forced to leave their small house in Tahlequah and now resided in a quite scruffy trailer in the woods near the Illinois River, just off Highway 62. But, as so often seems to be the case, the cliché applied that they were poor, but they were happy.

Aileen, who worked as many hours as she could get in a hair salon in Wagoner, not far from Tahlequah, had long harboured a wish to be a teacher. This was a wish that could never officially be fulfilled because of the lack of requisite qualifications, but it did come in useful when, almost inevitably, the teenage Alexander began to be an unreliable attender at school. It was a pain to get there, especially in winter, when a lengthy walk to the nearest road to pick up the school bus could be an unwelcome prospect in the early mornings. Aileen certainly didn't sanction these absences, which were followed up half-heartedly by the school authorities, but she did believe Alexander's pleas that he often felt unwell, with stomach pains and headaches. Please could he stay at home, just for today? Okay, just this once, dear, she would accept, realizing she would have to beg for extra shifts if she was to purchase more heating oil for the mobile home, which was isolated and could be bone-crackingly cold.

It was many years before the concept of home schooling became commonplace and monitored by education authorities, but in a way, Aileen and Alexander were pioneers in the field. Mathematics and particularly, literature were on the agenda, as Aileen made sure that the many absences from school were not to hinder Alexander's education. He never told her, but in later life he realized that the stomach cramps were most probably caused by the sneering comments of his classmates about his poor home and his ostracized father. Yes, his therapist in the eighties would confirm, you were suffering from stress.

This was the pattern for much of Alexander's teens. Most afternoons, Aileen would be collected by a work colleague for shifts at the salon, which would be the opportunity for her son to pick away at the various decrepit musical instruments his dad had left behind. Pino had claimed there was a rich musical tradition in his Native American background, but had shown little skill himself. Occasionally, as the alcoholism took hold, he had deluded himself with the hope that he might be able to make some cash by performing in the bars of north east Oklahoma, but the bitter reality was that he could hardly play and he certainly couldn't sing. Listening to Alexander, Aileen was surprised and gratified that maybe there was indeed a talent there, and that it had simply skipped a generation. It certainly wasn't from her side of the family - white middle class with no musical instruments anywhere near their home - and Aileen was pleased to give Alexander every encouragement.

The teenaged Alexander tried out the banjo but found it displeasingly harsh and unyielding, at least in his hands. But armed with his dad's ancient acoustic guitar and a harmonica in a holster he crafted himself from an old metal coat hanger, he could really fancy himself as a Bob Dylan figure, as he droned out folksy classics like "Down By The Riverside", "When The Saints Go Marching In" and "Oh Susanna". He struggled with finger picking, so his style ended up pretty much as the kind of strumming beyond which most people's guitar skills don't develop. He even tried his hand at writing a few songs of his own, using his limited arsenal of chords, but really, he didn't have much in the way of subject matter to work with. Aileen was impressed by these works of art and proud of her boy when he would play them to her on her return from work.

It was inevitable that Aileen would eventually meet a new man, and it brought a welcome change in circumstances to the small family. Lance Wilson was a friend of Aileen's boss and ran a small diner in the centre of Tahlequah, aimed at the motorists and tourists plying the historic road Route 66, which ran right through the town. Lance, not long divorced, was an astute businessman and all-round good guy, and before long, life in the apartment above the restaurant was a good deal more comfortable and convenient than it had been in the trailer in the woods. The trailer was sold to a dodgy-looking couple who would doubtless use it as a drug den, but then that wasn't the Cruz's problem any more.

Aileen was now in a position to do more shifts and Alexander, recently turned sixteen, was able to earn some cash as well, by means of the traditional rite-of-passage of burger-flipping. He was no longer required to attend high school but he had survived that long on account of being unobtrusive and co-operative on the occasions he'd been there. He certainly never caused any trouble and in the main, teachers had been impressed by how he had dealt with his unconventional upbringing. Half-hearted attempts to persuade him to stay on for further education after high school failed, because, having moved into town, Alex (as he was now, more coolly, known) was in the process of developing a social life.

Alex hadn't exactly been a loner, but living in the woods had made it hard to get out and about. Two other friends who had quit school at the same time as Alex were Jesse Allen and Mark Houghton. With a mutual interest in music, it was inevitable that they would form their first band together. Mark played fiddle, while both the others fancied themselves as guitarists. In the end, Alex conceded the more prominent rôle and agreed to teach himself double bass, on an ancient instrument that Lance Wilson bought for him from a second hand music shop in Tulsa.

Using the hours when the restaurant was closed, the trio christened themselves the Woodsmen in honour of Alex's old home and rehearsed enough folk songs to be able to get some (unpaid) gigs in a couple of the local bars. Using their dubious carpentry skills, they even constructed a makeshift stage in Lance's restaurant (which he predictably called Sir Lance-A-Lot). They built up quite a following as passing truckers and local drinkers chomped their Lanceburgers and swigged their Route 66 beer.

And then ... punk. Well, it happened to many bands around 1978. Not only were the Woodsmen planning to "go electric" and add drums, they were about to turn into a kind of band for which their particular corner of Oklahoma was unprepared. The way it came about was pretty fateful. A regular customer at Sir Lance-A-Lot, and indeed an occasional solo player there, was David Blue, drummer of a respected local soft-rock band called Bliss. It was David who told Alex about a show that Bliss had been booked for at Cain's Ballroom in Tulsa, opening for an English touring band. Would he like to come along for the ride? It promised to be something really special.

Alex was doubtful. Cain's Ballroom, while a legendary venue, was known for Western Swing, a type of music that the Woodsmen were trying to get away from. But the idea of being an honorary roadie for the night, carrying in David's drums and helping to set them up, was tempting. The date was January 11th 1978, the admission fee (from which Alex was excused on account of being "crew") was three dollars fifty, and the headlining band, "all the way from London, England" was the Sex Pistols. The following night, at the Winterland Ballroom in San Francisco, was to be the Pistols' last-ever gig, but no one knew that at the time.

Presumably, some of the people in attendance had known roughly what awaited them. Certainly, Alex and the band were well aware of punk. He'd read interviews with the Ramones in Rolling Stone and had already booked tickets to see them, due to play at Cain's a month later. The cool, high-energy rush of bands like the Ramones and the New York Dolls was appealing to the teenage Woodsmen, feeling pretty isolated in their geographical and cultural backwater. Without the offer of a lift and a free ticket, Alex probably wouldn't have bothered with the Sex Pistols, as their reputation for chaotic live shows didn't appeal to the musician in him, even though this was their first (and, as it turned out, only) American tour.

The band's reputation had preceded them, and outside the quaint ballroom, quite a large crowd of banner-waving, bible-punching protesters had gathered in the road. Rural Oklahoma was a conservative and deeply Christian environment. One of the banners read, "Life is 'Rotten' Without God's Only Begotten Jesus."

The audience was an uneasy mix of punk followers, the normal Cain's audience and the merely curious, some seeking trouble. There were also a number of journalists from national music magazines, and a smattering of undercover police, on the alert for any potentially lewd behaviour onstage. Alex was unaware of any of this, armed with a backstage pass and dutifully carrying in the drums in the freezing conditions; Bliss had barely made it to Tulsa though the snow.

The Pistols had arrived early. They'd driven overnight from Dallas, partly to combat the bad weather and partly because Johnny Rotten had allegedly smashed a Texan reporter's camera and they were concerned about his wrath and the police's. Bliss weren't granted access to the Pistols' dressing room, but they could hear them living up to their reputation, swearing and being contemptuous of any questions they were asked. Bliss performed a short and largely ignored set, and Alex was out front when the Pistols came onstage and blasted into their show. It was loud, it was rough and ready, but it certainly wasn't chaotic in any unintended way. Like millions of other youths the world over, Alex had his life changed that evening, as Johnny Rotten leered into the microphone, Sid Vicious snarled and sneered, and Steve Jones studiously ignored an entire pitcher of beer that was thrown over him. This wasn't just hype, it was pure excitement.

Afterwards, Alex witnessed Vicious and Rotten stubbing out cigarettes on their arms as their fee was counted out to them by venue manager Scott Munz, who was later quoted in the local press as considering them "blasphemous, provocative and irreverent". These were all attributes which appealed to young Alex, and when he described his evening out to the other Woodsmen, the band's change of direction became a matter of course. Within weeks, Alex had switched to electric bass, amps had been bought (Mark built his own cabinet), a drummer had been recruited, Jesse had switched from fiddle to electric guitar and the band name had been changed.

Was it arrogance, provocation or youthful idiocy which led them to christen themselves The Chocs? Jesse, too, had a Choctaw family background and the name sounded to them both snappy and memorable. From a publicity point of view in the era of punk, they couldn't have done better, but as soon as the first gig posters appeared (their slogan was "Chocs Away!"), there was outrage in the community. The Oklahoma Choctaw Historical Society declared it a slur on their traditions, while the Tahlequah Daily Press called for the group to be banned. In music business terms, it was a PR triumph: scandal and notoriety before the first gig had been played.

Checking out a rehearsal, in which he discovered that the cheery folk tunes had been replaced by aggressive, three-minute shoutalongs, Lance politely made clear that his restaurant would not be a suitable place for them to make their début. Business was tough at the best of times, and he certainly couldn't afford a potential boycott. Although keen to support her son's efforts, Aileen agreed, so the Chocs' first gig took place at a local college (where the principal insisted they were billed merely as "special guests", to avoid the posters causing further offence). Apart from a few scuffles and some derogatory comments from some of the male students, who didn't like their girlfriends checking out the guys' newly-purchased skinny jeans, it went well enough to generate the beginnings of a following. There was certainly no competition in the way of other punk bands in town.

Modelling themselves vaguely on the Ramones, the Chocs died their hair black and, doing their own bookings, played anywhere they could in the area. Playing various local roadhouses, they were generally received with hostility, but this merely helped to enhance their anti-establishment reputation. There were a few higher-profile gigs in places like Eureka Springs, over the border in Arkansas, and the Crystal Pistol, the newly-established punk venue in Tulsa. They even pitched for the Patti Smith Band support slot back at Cain's Ballroom, but it was already taken. It was at one of their Crystal Pistol shows that they met Larry Goldberg, who was to become their manager and sign them to his Stud record label.

Larry fancied himself as in the same mould as Seymour Stein, the founder of Sire Records. Respected for his maverick personality and ability to find quirky and original new wave acts, Stein had built up a successful empire and Larry Goldberg planned to emulate him. He was actually a New Yorker but was visiting friends in Tulsa that night, and had read a news item in the local paper about the Chocs being pulled over on the highway on suspicion of dope possession. Nothing had been found, but the cops had allegedly pushed them around a bit and spoken to them demeaningly. Alex's mum Aileen, by now becoming quite enthused about the following the Chocs were building, had written to a journalist under a pseudonym, complaining of victimization. This led to a nice piece of publicity for the band.

The police were probably a bit out of date in what they were searching for. Most of the hippie groups they were used to would undoubtedly have had a stash of weed somewhere in their van, but the Chocs were a high-energy band and needed to do a lot of late-night driving, so speed was their chosen stimulant. There were almost certainly some little pills flicked out of the window onto the grass verge as they were being pulled over. No matter, they got their piece in the paper and Larry Goldberg came to their gig.

It wasn't particularly Larry's style of music, but he was an astute impresario and could see which way the wind was blowing musically. The Chocs fitted the mould nicely and the next morning, over coffee in Lance's bar, he offered the band a deal.

"Listen, boys, I can take you out of here and make you into stars."

It was such a cliché that it was almost laughable, but the Chocs were willing, and – let's face it – naïve victims.

"You mean we'll be able to travel all over the world?"

"Sure thing. You guys are the future of the music business."

A few days later, the contract arrived in the post. Cautiously, Aileen asked a lawyer friend to look it over. The friend was actually a real estate expert and found it hard to work his way through the dense music business legal terminology such as "points" and "redeemable but not recoupable", but nevertheless declared that it seemed "all right". All the song publishing was assigned to Larry. With local friends as witnesses, all four members signed the contract. Cue joy. It hardly seemed possible.

Larry had a record producer friend who had a studio in Oklahoma City, and, after a few weeks working on arrangements and rehearsing, the Chocs came up with ten songs which they considered representative, almost all of them three-minute rants with few chords, and therefore relatively easy to record. The line-up was now the classic rock group configuration: Two guitars, bass and drums. For the album title, "Rock With The Chocs" was rejected by consensus as naff and replaced by the hardly less naff "Don't Knock The Chocs" - seen as having echoes of "Never Mind The Bollocks". The song chosen for a single was the one which least represented their style - a stadium-style rock anthem called "Mad And Bad", written by Alex, with a singalong chorus inaccurately plagiarized from John Lydon. The day after Alex had seen the Sex Pistols, they had played their last ever show, in San Francisco. Johnny Rotten famously signed off with the question, "Ever get the feeling you've been cheated?" In Alex's song, it came out like this:

"Ever get the feeling you've been had? Baby baby, I'm mad and I'm bad."

No one had jobs they were committed to, so when Larry recommended relocating en masse to New York, the Chocs were up for it in a big way. The loft apartment they were installed in seemed to be mysteriously rent-free. It was a long time before they realized that this was just one of the many items being put down by Larry as recoupable expenses, but for the time being, life was sweet. Larry's contacts book was strong enough to secure them a residency at the legendary CBGBs and regular shows at other significant New York venues. When he sent them on a coast-to-coast tour, all meals and motels were paid for even though the fees at the murky fleapit venues they played were tiny. The euphoria when "Mad And Bad", on the Stud label, peaked at number 42 in the Billboard charts on the back of an interview in Rolling Stone and a healthy amount of radio airplay, was enough to make the Chocs feel they had truly arrived. Back in Tahlequah, the Daily Press suddenly had a new attitude to them: "Chocs Away! Local band storms US charts."

Alex expressed quiet satisfaction to his mother.

"I thought I could write songs, Mom, and now I've proved it."

Although he normally co-wrote the band's songs with Jesse, "Mad And

Bad" had been a solo effort, a throw-away idea, really. Alex was confident that the songwriting royalties would soon start to flow.

"I'll share it with the other guys, Larry, they deserve a cut too."

"Yep, it won't be long before the cheques will start to arrive."

In the meantime, however, all four Chocs were busy being very stupid and above all, in the tradition of young, naïve rock groups, boringly predictable. Cocaine was de rigeur for almost all rock bands at the time, but not everyone went further. Alex was foolish, but, in his defence, many young musicians of that era really had no idea what they were getting themselves into. He first tried freebasing crack in the Château Marmont Hotel in LA after a gig at the Whiskey A-Go-Go. The singer of the headline band told him he just had to give it a go, and wouldn't believe the high that could be achieved. Everybody was doing it, even venerable elder statesmen of rock like David Crosby, so it didn't seem much more significant than slamming down a Tequila. The band members' consequent mood swings and volatile behaviour (all the Chocs indulged to varying degrees apart from Mark, and even he developed an alcohol problem) meant that further fame or fortune were doomed never to materialize. Their live performances became unreliable, their second single made no ripples and "Don't Knock the Chocs" was a sitting duck for the barbed-pen music critics, who gave it a royal trouncing as naïve and derivative.

An inability to deal with drugs wasn't the only rock 'n' roll feature of Alex's personality. He indulged enthusiastically in the delights of the flesh too. The groupie scene offered itself to him and he certainly wasn't going to decline. But sometimes, he would take liberties which went beyond casual sex. On one occasion, in Detroit, he had to get out of town fast when a furious father with a gun was after him for allegedly going too far with an under-age girl who had resisted his advances. He'd misunderstood her flirtatious behaviour as being an invitation for sex, and didn't like it when she was reluctant. "I thought she was asking for it," he told the other Chocs.

The cool intelligentsia of the New York music scene had no place for these literal hicks from the sticks, so it wasn't really a surprise when, in March 1981, they were called to Larry Goldberg's Manhattan office.

That was the day when the Chocs realized that they really should have looked into their contract in more detail. The second album which they had been looking forward to recording turned out merely to be an "option", that Larry could have taken up if he'd wanted to. The publishing rights for their songs rested with Larry too, with only a tiny percentage due to the writers, and in any case, any royalties due from record sales or publishing had long since been eaten up by their day-to-day expenses.

"Boys, you have no idea how much I've invested in this project."

"But we're the ones who've done all the work."

"Without me, you'd never have had the work in the first place. You've had a great time, you've travelled all over the States, you've been on the radio, you've even had a hit record. If it wasn't for me, you'd still be doing dead-end jobs in Tahlequah. But the time has come where I've got to cut my losses. I'm sorry, boys."

The way Larry presented it, he'd been doing the band a massive favour by enabling them to pursue their brief career.

For the three other Chocs, it was the end of an adventure they'd never really planned in the first place. Mark, Jesse and drummer Brian returned to their families in Oklahoma, got jobs and continued to play local venues in amateur bands. Alex, however, decided to stay in New York, because he had fallen in love.

While attending an acoustic show in the Bottom Line club, Alex had got chatting with the girl doing the door. Molly was a pretty art student and also a part-time musician who was aware that Alex had been a member of a "signed" band. Before long, they were partners in life (Alex moved into Molly's tiny apartment in the Bowery), in music (they started writing and performing together) and yes, in crime (they bonded over a shared interest in hard drugs, specifically heroin, onto which Alex had moved in the wake of the band's split-up). The couple eked out an existence doing poorly paid support slots as an acoustic duo, but that wasn't enough to live on.

Their reputation around town became that of a surrogate Sid Vicious and Nancy Spungen, as they eventually ended up emulating the likes of Peter Perrett and Johnny Thunders in a sordid lifestyle funded by their own dealing. That old cliché about how you have to hit rock bottom before starting to climb back held true for the pair, who were struggling to cope when their baby daughter, Lucy, was born in October 1983.

Keen to meet her granddaughter, and unaware of the lifestyle change that had affected her son, Aileen drove all the way to New York to bring the young family home to Tahlequah for Christmas. That something was wrong soon became obvious. Unmistakable clues were a lethargic baby, a mother who kept dozing off, and a father who had to make regular trips to visit unidentified "friends", usually late at night. All those fears about what might befall her son in the Big City seemed to have been justified.

Things had been looking up for Aileen and Lance. They'd gone into business together and their Sir Lance-A-Lot brand had expanded into a small chain of outlets; the concept of burgers and live music had caught on. Shocked and ashamed at what had befallen Alex, Lance was at least in a financial position to offer his adopted son and his new family a spell in a local rehab facility. Feeling less anxious back in his childhood environment, Alex was in a good position to summon up the willpower required, but Molly's attempts at withdrawal soon petered out.

The lure of heroin was so strong that, after a few weeks, she opted to return to New York and the oblivion it offered. Against all advice, and contrary to Alex's wishes, Molly took the infant Lucy with her, but it wasn't long before Lance again had to head up to the Big Apple to retrieve the child. After a couple of months, poor Molly was dead, found slumped in the rest-room of a New York bar after taking an overdose. Nobody knew whether it was intentional or not.

With Alex away in rehab, Aileen unexpectedly found herself being a mother again – this time to her granddaughter. Little Lucy, often parked in a buggy in the office from where Aileen administered the Lance-A-Lot empire, gradually regained health. Alex took months to get over the death of Molly, but in a way the pointlessness of it galvanized him, until he was eventually able to resume fatherly duties and effectively start his "solo career", touring the Lance-A-Lot chain with an acoustic guitar, doing a set of originals and a few covers by the likes of Leonard Cohen and Elvis Costello. The climax of each show was, inevitably, a singalong version of "Mad And Bad", the nearest thing Oklahoma had to a state anthem until, many years later, the Flaming Lips released "Do You Realize?"

Unsurprisingly, the lyrical preoccupations of Alex's songs tended to centre around the torment of withdrawal, the cruel vagaries of the music business, the agony of lost love and the joys of fatherhood. A second try at stardom wasn't on the agenda until Green On Red hit Oklahoma City in mid-1985. Country rock and its indie branch-offs had attracted Alex's interest and his set already contained Byrds and REM covers, so he drove over to see the pioneering Los Angeles band, classified by the press as part of the "Paisley Underground", having been joined in 1985 by Chuck Prophet for the "Gas Food Lodging" album. In a corridor after the gig, Alex bumped into Green On Red's front man Dan Stuart and their brief conversation about music was enough to convince Alex that his next step would be to form a psychedelic country rock band back in Tahlequah.

From the original Chocs, both Jesse and Mark were interested. Alex purchased a 12-string Rickenbacker and switched from bass to lead guitar. A drummer called Will Sharp was recruited via a notice in the local music store, and once again, the search was on for a name. This time, it was easier and less controversial. Gram Parsons was the acknowledged king of country rock and "gram" was a drug measurement, so The Grams was a cool name with all the requisite rock and roll connotations.

Things moved fast. The country rock that the Grams were doing chimed exactly with what the music industry required at that moment, and by mid-1986, they had completed tours supporting REM and the Dream Syndicate and also been signed by a proper label, a subsidiary of A & M. Their first album, "Desert Grave", largely written by Alex, while not charting, hit all the right notes with publications such as Melody Maker and NME in the UK. They even made the front cover of "Sounds", although not with a photo, just a flash heralding an interview on page 6.

Ironically, despite being recognized far more in Europe than in the US, they never got to tour over there, partly for financial reasons and partly due to managerial incompetence. The Grams were dropped in 1990, having only got as far as demoing their second album but not recording it. They hadn't hit major headlining status, but they had certainly achieved respectability. Sales, however, were more important to the record company than the much-coveted kudos of a "cult following". But without that cult following, Corey Zander would never have reached Wikipedia.

Alex's friends had called him Zander for years, and Corey Zander was his idea of a cool country rock name. He adopted it when the Grams were signed, partly to avoid unwelcome comparisons with the Chocs, and partly to draw a line under his previous espousal of the darker side of rock and roll. The Grams were a band that was entirely free of hard drugs, although none of them were averse to the odd slug of bourbon to help out with onstage confidence, and calming joints were a familiar feature of the dressing room.

The Grams had spent time in Los Angeles and San Francisco, but their base had always been in North East Oklahoma. Thus, Corey (as he was forever henceforth to be known) remained close to his daughter Lucy, with Aileen helping out when the band was on tour. But many of the musicians Corey was meeting on the road hailed either from Nashville or Austin, Texas. Corey felt that Nashville was probably a bit "straight country" for him, but Austin, the self-appointed "live music capital of the world", was an alluring prospect.

Still not comfortable with the prevalent right-leaning, church-orientated ethos of Tahlequah, Corey was intrigued by tales of this liberal-minded University city where music was king. Austin, so he was told, was home to hundreds of music venues and like-minded blues and roots musicians such as Stevie Ray Vaughan (the most famous), along with the likes of Joe Ely, Doug Sahm, of course, Willie Nelson. It sounded very much like the kind of place he'd like Lucy to grow up in.

He "relocated" there (something Americans seemed to do with ease and regularity) in 1991, starting a new life with Lucy, who grew up in a laid-back atmosphere near the bohemian South Congress area, filled with music bars and art galleries. It was not surprising that Lucy would become both a musician and an artist.

When Ben Walker, back in Winchester, was approached by the UK agent Glenn Wallis, he was told that Corey Zander was one of the more respected musicians in Austin, having been a minor luminary of the scene there for over twenty years. He regularly played legendary music haunts such as the Saxon Pub and the Cactus Café, on bills including the likes of Alejandro Escovedo and James McMurtry. Ben was aware of the Grams and knew that plenty of Austin musicians, many of them ex-members of well-known bands, regularly toured Europe as solo artists. The audiences they drew tended to be respectable, if not large, but he was attracted by the "exclusivity" of the fact that Corey had never toured the UK before. So when approached by Glenn Wallis, Ben had said, "What the heck, let's give it a go" and wandered up to The Station to enquire about putting on a show. But as he struggled with the lack of ticket sales and the non-existent publicity, he was painfully aware of a sensation of having bitten off more than he could chew.

Chapter 3

It was Saturday afternoon and Ben was listening to a play on Radio Four as he pulled onto the M3 towards Heathrow to meet Corey Zander off the plane from Houston. He wondered what exactly awaited him, certain that, whatever it was, it would be a person with whom he could surely have little in common. Ben's upbringing had been dramatically different to that of the man he was about to meet.

Ben was an only child, brought up in the pleasant village of Chew Magna, near Bristol, in south-west England. His father Brian was an accountant, earning sufficiently well for it to be unnecessary for his mother Joanna to have a day job, although she did plenty of charity work.

Attending the local comprehensive school, Ben was an unremarkable young man. He wasn't excessively sporty or intelligent or naughty, just a run-of-the-mill kid from a stable family who was always destined for a middle-of-the-road job in local government or a school. He progressed through GCSEs and A-levels and ended up studying English at Birmingham University, where he attained a 2-1.

Following the pattern of all those who don't know what to do with their lives, Ben enrolled on a postgraduate teacher training course in Southampton, and was 24 by the time he took up his first teaching post in a primary school in Winchester. He'd been there for three years by the time he decided to take his plunge into gig promotion.

How had he ended up in Winchester? On his PGCE course in Southampton, he'd met Rosie, in her last year of an estate management course at the nearby Solent University. The two of them got on well, going jogging together in Southampton's parks and enjoying evenings at the Nuffield Theatre. They joined a ukulele group at the Platform Tavern and spent Wednesday evenings strumming away.

By the end of the year, Ben and Rosie were an item and she had fixed him up with a job at Saint John's Primary School in Winchester, where her father Robert Leighton was the head teacher. Strictly speaking, it hadn't been nepotism, and there had been a procedure involving advertising the post and interviewing various other hapless candidates who had travelled long distances in the hope of securing the job. Effectively, though, Rosie had in fact "fixed" it, because Robert knew that Ben was his daughter's boyfriend and that her greatest wish was for him to settle down with her in her home town. Rosie, in turn, quickly got a post with Poole's estate agency, one of the many property companies lining the ancient city's Southgate Street.

Eighteen months after graduating, the couple announced their engagement, much to the delight of their families. In a suburb called Weeke, they bought an ex-council owned one-bedroom maisonette (a posh word for a flat). Even with both of them on reasonable salaries, this was all they could afford in this most expensive corner of the UK and even then, they were mortgaged to the maximum, with no money to spare (Rosie would have pointed out, if she'd known) for risky forays into concert promotion when what they really should be doing was saving for the wedding. Ben wasn't quite so sure. While he'd had a couple of flings at university in Birmingham, Rosie was his first proper girlfriend and, when he had time to think about it (primary teaching being a very demanding job), he did fear that he was drifting into something he wasn't quite ready for. Since leaving university, they had spent most of their time together and seemed the perfect couple, but their lives were dissimilar in certain ways.

Rosie tended to hang out with people involved in the property business, whose main topic of conversation was the price of houses. She didn't really share Ben's rapidly developing obsession with "Americana" music, and his love of bands such as Midlake, the Low Anthem and Grandaddy. The previous autumn, Ben had gone, on his own, to the End Of The Road Festival near Salisbury and seen all three of those bands, as well as some solo American performers like Charlie Parr and Malcolm Holcombe, both of whom were quite similar in style to what he expected from Corey

Zander. Rosie had shown little interest in coming to the festival, but neither of them thought there was anything wrong or unusual in having differing hobbies.

It only took an hour for Ben to reach Heathrow. Monday's gig at The Station was to be the first show of Corey Zander's European tour, which was, as Ben had vainly hoped the newspapers would trumpet, "Corey Zander's first ever UK performance." This meant that Corey would need accommodation for three nights. Hotel prices in Winchester were astronomical and not even the local Travelodges had any special offers on. With their flat being too small (Rosie absolutely drew the line at allowing Corey to sleep on her sofa), an unlikely solution had been attained, whereby Corey would stay with Robert the headmaster/potential father-in-law and his wife Diana in one of the spare bedrooms of their large home in the affluent Chilbolton Avenue area of Winchester. It was a generous offer, and one which Ben had no reason to worry about; after all, his research had shown that Corey Zander had long since left his hell-raising days behind him, living a quiet life in downtown Austin with his now 29-year-old daughter Lucy.

Ben parked optimistically in the Short Stay car park at Terminal Four and joined the phalanxes of card-brandishing taxi drivers waiting at Arrivals. He'd printed out an A4 sheet saying C. ZANDER and used the school laminator to make it look more official. And there he stood, for over an hour and a half after the monitors had declared that flight AA 493 from Houston had LANDED. Uh-oh. What if Corey had missed the flight or simply got cold feet? He hadn't even got any contact details. His stomach, already swishing from three Costa cappuccinos, began to sprout butterflies.

Corey, when he arrived, looked angry. Very, very angry. Even having watched a couple of You Tube live videos filmed in Antone's Club in Austin, Ben was unprepared for the vision which assailed him. Among the suited businessmen and bronzed holidaymakers streaming into the arrivals area, Corey stood out a mile. For a start, bearing in mind that he'd once been a skinny-jeaned Ramones clone, he was fat, a large belly extending over a silver cowhorn-buckled belt that held up a battered pair of droopy-arsed Levi's. His jacket was a grey lumberjack affair.

"Thank Christ he isn't wearing a Davy Crockett hat," thought Ben, although the reality was nearly as bad. As well as a heavy-looking rucksack, Corey was carrying a battered sticker-covered guitar case and his headgear was an ancient leather Stetson, making him look something like an extra from "Once Upon A Time In The West". And then there was the beard.

Ben had vaguely expected - indeed feared - a bear hug in the traditional American style, but Corey was in no mood for embraces. "Motherfuckers" was his first word by way of greeting.

"Have you had problems?"

"It was my fucking beard, I know it was."

It was indeed an impressive beard, reaching chest level and culminating in three miniature pigtails. Ben could surmise what had happened. The previous year, returning from holiday, he'd spotted the Texan songwriter Josh T. Pearson being stopped at border control in Gatwick, merely on account of his luxuriant chin furniture. The border officers clearly didn't realize that any travellers planning on drug smuggling or similar activities would try to make themselves as unobtrusive as possible. Instead, their policy was to pull over anyone who looked a bit weird, and Corey, of course, fitted the bill admirably.

"They kept me waiting for over an hour, just because of my beard, and then they impounded all my merch."

"Merch?"

"My CDs. I brought a hundred CDs with me and they stole the lot."

The agent had told Ben that CD sales were the main source of income for anyone from the US on tour in Europe, so this was bad news for Corey.

"Where were they?"

"In my suitcase. They said I can pick them up when I leave the country, or pay £250 duty to bring them in."

"But didn't you tell them you needed to sell them?"

"I don't have a work permit. I said they were promotional items to give away to friends, but they didn't believe me."

This was a real shame, thought Ben. He'd been sent an advance copy of the new album, "Live At The Saxon Pub" and it was, indeed, a very good record, dark, brooding and confessional: just the sort of thing Americana fans would love. He thought fast.

"If I pay the £250, will you guarantee to pay it back as soon as you've sold 25 CDs?" His flesh crept as he imagined Rosie's reaction were she to discover he'd been playing fast and loose with their meagre savings. "But for Christ's sake, don't tell my fiancée."

Another hour later, and with the help of Ben's credit card, the roll-along suitcase had been refilled with the boxes of CDs. With alarm, Ben noticed that the only other things in the case were a toothbrush and a few pairs of socks and underpants. Corey clearly planned to do his entire UK tour in the clothes he stood up in. The conversation with the border officials had to be a very guarded affair. The lack of work permit was something Ben hadn't considered, so he had to pretend that Corey was an old friend coming to visit him and not on any account make any reference to gigs. Recently, a Canadian singer had been deported when found to be working without permission. Border Agency officials had marched her offstage in the middle of a performance in a pub in Swindon, driven her to Dover and put her on a ferry to France.

By the time they were cruising past Fleet Services on the M3 in the rain, Corey had calmed down a lot. He was grateful, he said, to Ben for meeting him, accommodating him and bailing him out. How strange it was to drive on the left and how quaintly English the rain was. Ben, in turn, described his excitement at putting on Corey's first UK show, although it was just possible, he warned, that not many people would be there. He also explained why Corey would be staying with his fiancée's parents.

It was dark when they pulled into the driveway of Robert and Diana's detached house. The courtesy light flickered on and no doubt the curtains twitched in the adjacent properties as the wheels of the heavy suitcase carved out grooves in the gravel. Both the prospective in-laws were out for Saturday dinner with friends so Ben showed Corey to his room.

"I'm jet-lagged," declared Corey. "See you tomorrow."

He disappeared into the room and Ben headed home, where Rosie was reading the Weekly News property supplement and didn't really want to be bothered with stories of beards and borders. Ben cracked open a can of Fosters from the fridge, grabbed a packet of Kettle chips and lay down on the sofa in front of a recording of "Later With Jools Holland". So far, he thought, apart from his credit card bill, so good.

The plan for the Sunday was to take the guest for a tour of Winchester. Surely, any foreign visitor was bound to be fascinated by the grave of Jane Austen in the cathedral, the statue of King Alfred in the Broadway and the Round Table of the mythical King Arthur in the Great Hall of Winchester Castle. After that, maybe a walk round the local beauty spot of Farley Mount would prove that English autumn leaves could put on a display to rival anything America could offer. Finally, late Sunday roast, a uniquely British proposition, could be eaten in the eccentric city pub The Black Boy.

But it didn't work out like that. When Ben arrived with Rosie at Chilbolton Avenue in the late morning, the in-laws were looking concerned.

"We didn't know whether to wake him," explained Diana. "We haven't heard a sound."

"He's had a long journey and a lot of stress. He's probably jet-lagged. Let's just leave him."

The afternoon was spent helping Robert to sweep up leaves and catching up with some episodes from a boxed set of "Downton Abbey", and it was evening before Corey emerged, seemingly having not even undressed. He accepted Ben's offer of tea, although he asked for honey in it ("good for my voice"). Robert and Diana had already left to visit Diana's mother, who lived in Chandler's Ford and had recently left hospital after an operation. They were intending to stay the night there, leaving the coast free for Ben to play host to this bizarre intruder. This left just Ben, Corey and Rosie and a slightly awkward lack of conversation. Having explained the practicalities of the gig, as far as he understood them, and asked all about Austin (receiving minimal information in response), Ben had run out of things to say. Corey showed no interest in the copy of the International Herald Tribune which Ben had purchased because, bizarrely, it was on Corey's rider document. Rosie, meanwhile, had absolutely nothing in common with a person she plainly saw as an intruder and was merely, quite obviously, repelled by him.

Corey abruptly stood up, opened the front door and disappeared. This was something Ben had been waiting for with apprehension. During the drug-fuelled and volatile days of The Chocs, Corey had been renowned for his habit of "doing a runner". On one well-documented occasion, he'd taken exception to something Jesse said to him on stage at the Doug Fir Lounge in Portland, Oregon and had hurled down his bass, walked out of the main entrance and simply kept on walking. He'd been found the following morning miles away, down among the homeless people beside the Willamette River, asleep on a park bench. But surely, those days were long in the past?

Within an hour, Corey was back, and he had a question.

"Hey Ben, do you have any blow?"

Ben was speechless. Not only had he been certain that Corey's drug days were long over, he had absolutely no idea where, in this provincial town, he could lay his hands on any dope. The circles he moved in, where mild-mannered teachers went about their daily work, hardly featured even beer, let alone any illegal substances. Parts of Winchester, according to the Weekly News, did have a drug culture, but it certainly didn't impinge on Ben's or Rosie's lives, and the nature of his job meant that Ben wasn't inclined to offer Corey any help.

"Er ... no, I'm afraid not."

"Can you get hold of any? I've tried, but no one knows where to go."

Ben's blood ran cold. Please God, don't say Corey has been knocking on the well-heeled doors of Chilbolton Avenue asking people if they could sell him marihuana?

"Where have you tried?"

"I went down the road. I tried the kebab shop, the Albion and the Old Gaolhouse."

Good grief! The Old Gaolhouse was a Wetherspoon's drinking den. Maybe some of the clientèle would have access to dope, but, unlike, perhaps, the free and easy atmosphere of Austin, Texas, in Winchester you didn't just wander into pubs and randomly ask people for drugs, especially if you looked like a grizzly backwoodsman.

"Corey, you're lucky to have got into the country at all, and now you're already risking being deported. This is a small town. Robert is a head teacher and if word gets out he is playing host to a drug user, he'll probably be fired. Besides, I thought you'd given up drugs."

Corey laughed. "I have, but a bit of blow isn't drugs. I need it to relax. I can't play without it, I get too nervous. I thought it would be easy to find some. Are you sure you don't have any friends who can help?"

Ben sighed, incredulous that he got himself involved in something already out of control. Thank goodness, Rosie was in the other room, uploading some house details onto Pooles' website ready for the next day. The only person Ben could think of was Jim, a friend who had been on the PGCE course with him at Southampton but had dropped out. Ben knew that Jim and his wife liked the occasional joint; he'd seen them lighting up after a recent dinner party. He took out his iPhone and dialled Jim's number.

"It's not for me, of course," he found himself saying, truthfully. Jim assured him he could help. Ben showed Corey where the Bourbon was (another rider item, along with the honey, salsa and olives, stored in a cardboard box in the hallway) and set off to meet Jim at his flat in the Portswood area of Southampton. Actually getting his hands on the stuff entailed making a lengthy trip with Jim in a dark, rickety and graffiti-covered elevator to the top of a shabby tower block in Millbrook and paying a dodgy-looking dreadlocked guy called Carl twenty quid for something that seemed like a large toffee wrapped in cellophane. Carl was just as Ben had imagined a drug dealer would be like, unfriendly and not at all interested in the genial banter that Ben attempted, trying to make it seem as if he knew what he was doing. On the drive back, feeling lucky to be alive, something approaching panic overtook Ben. What to other people would have had absolutely no significance (Jim thought Ben's worries were hilarious) was a massive deal for Ben. He was a TEACHER, and here he was, procuring illegal drugs to be consumed in the house of someone who was a respected HEADMASTER and, what was more, his future FATHER-IN-LAW. Oh God.

It was late when Ben got back to Chilbolton Avenue and furtively handed over the goods.

"Thanks, man," was Corey's response, as he ambled out on to the decking by the garden shed, filled a little hash pipe he had in his pocket and lit up. How the hell had he got THAT through customs? They must have been obsessed with the CDs. Rosie had gone home, so, begging Corey to leave no traces, Ben was about to leave him to it.

"Do you have this guy's phone number?" asked Corey.

"What guy?"

"The guy you got this stuff from."

"But Corey, you'd never find the place."

"No worries. I can call him and he can deliver."

Ben sighed and gave him Carl's mobile number. He was fed up with this. Tomorrow was a work day and he'd pick up Corey late Monday afternoon to take him to the gig. Rosie was asleep when he got home, having curiously not left him the traditional note on the kitchen table, detailing various jobs he needed to do.

Chapter 4

Ben wasn't sure he'd chosen the right career. In fact, he feared he might be going through a very premature midlife crisis. He had 28 children in his Year Four class at St John's School and often, the responsibility felt overwhelming. He wasn't sure whether his feelings constituted panic attacks, but he spent much of each day feeling nauseous, unable to focus and mildly dizzy. The children (eight and nine-year-olds) were permanently in motion, constantly demanding his attention. Their middle-class parents were always requiring him to detail their children's exact levels of progress and sort out their myriad relationship problems with other pupils. As an English graduate, Ben struggled to deliver a curriculum which demanded that he teach every subject, including maths and science, areas which were so alien to him that he felt barely more knowledgeable than his pupils. This meant that hours had to be spent every evening preparing lessons.

Government regulations required a large amount of record keeping. Preparing pupils for their "Standard Attainment Tests", teachers had to produce copious details on the exact progress of each child. But the pressure wasn't only on him. Primary schools were judged and rated on the results of tests, and this meant considerable stress for Robert, the headmaster. If standards fell, particularly in a smart area like this, information would be published in the local press, parents would possibly choose another school, numbers would fall and jobs could be threatened.

None of this would have mattered so much were it not for the fact that, as it stood, Ben would soon be related to Robert. This personal connection made for a strange dynamic in their relationship. It was not unusual for them to be sharing dinner one night and having a tetchy formal meeting the next day. "I'm sorry to have to say this, Ben, but I'm afraid you're going to have to pull yourself together ..."

Teachers earned their money all right. If he'd been willing to devote every waking hour to the job, Ben would probably have been able to keep up with all the form-filling and record-keeping, the playground duties and the extra-curricular activities. But he didn't really like the job enough to show such dedication, and he wasn't that keen on Robert either. Cowed by the system and coming from a more conservative generation, Robert was the kind of grey-suited, grey-minded career educationalist responsible for squeezing all the fun out of working with children. The sort of creative activities that Ben enjoyed so much, such as singing and drama, had been virtually eliminated from the school day. For Ben, it had effectively reached the stage where he was only doing the job for the pay cheque.

Ben's love of music, and the "Americana" genre in particular, was pretty much his only hobby. He loved Neil Young and Tom Waits and tried to keep up with new artists too. He'd been to Shepherds Bush Empire to see Laura Veirs and to the Queen Elizabeth Hall for Lucinda Williams. Rosie was quite happy with it but didn't share his obsession, so Ben's musical enjoyment was confined to his iPod and headphones, and his trips to concerts were solo activities. Rosie, meanwhile, would hang out with her friends in the property business. Most of her colleagues were married and she looked forward to tying the knot with Ben within the next year. They had already talked about having children. They got on well domestically, but the truth was that they didn't actually see a huge amount of each other. In the evenings, Ben was either out at a gig or a parents' evening, or else marking piles of exercise books and writing reports.

Ben didn't really have a lot of time for his putative mother-in-law Diana. With her dyed blonde hair, her expensive clothes and her gigantic 4x4, she was the archetypal "lady who lunches". She did part-time charity work for the Samaritans (sometimes Ben would fear the scenario were he to need their help and unwittingly get Diana on the end of the line), and also dabbled in property, having bought a couple of flats in town and rented them out to students at the university. She lived a life of carefree comfort and wished for the same for her daughter. The sooner Ben got promoted, married Rosie and they settled down, the better. Diana had offered to give Ben and Rosie money to buy their flat, but Ben had refused, saying he wasn't prepared to accept charity. This caused considerable friction. It was hard to understand how Diana could live such a life as the wife of a primary head teacher, but Ben worked out that she must have inherited money from her wealthy parents. She exuded the calm, uncomprehending confidence of the well-off.

All in all, it was pretty sporting of this conventional couple to agree to accommodate Corey Zander. Ben had, however, been slightly economical with the truth, going no further than describing him as "a friend of a friend from America". If they'd had an inkling that he was smoking dope on their patio, they'd have had a nervous breakdown, probably even called the police. In fact, by the time Ben collected him from their house on Monday afternoon, they still hadn't actually clapped eyes on him. Nonetheless, Robert agreed to come along to the show, and to help out if necessary. Diana had her bridge evening, so had to "reluctantly" decline. Rosie pluckily said she'd help Ben by selling and checking tickets at the door. They knew that the success of the evening meant a great deal to Ben.

It was a trying day at school. Ben, on the day of his first attempt at concert promoting, was fretting and concentrating on anything other than the welfare of his little darlings. When tested to the limit by one girl who wouldn't stop asking his opinion of a Halloween picture she'd drawn, he shouted at her and made her cry. At 3.30, therefore, when he'd planned to rush off and attend to the welfare of Corey Zander, he had to deal with a wrathful mother at the school gates, whose daughter had told her he'd been mean to her. It was nearly five by the time Ben got to Chilbolton Avenue.

In the chilly autumn sunshine, Corey was sitting on the leaf-strewn patio, as if he hadn't moved since the night before, although he assured Ben that he'd been to bed.

"Have you seen Diana?"

"Sure, she's real sweet. She made me bacon and eggs and gave me tea with honey. I played her a few songs and then she went to lunch and isn't back yet."

It's a miracle, thought Ben. Somehow, Corey Zander had clearly worked his charms on Diana, at least to the extent that she hadn't run screaming to the neighbours. And there he sat, acoustic guitar in hand, in the process of compiling a set list.

"Do you like Indian food?" asked Ben.

"Can't say I've tried it, but why not?"

"Okay, shall we head to the venue now?"

"I'm as ready as I'll ever be."

Arriving at The Station was a dispiriting experience. For a start, the place was locked and it took 15 minutes of knocking to elicit a response from landlord Andy, who had clearly been having a late afternoon nap. The place stank of stale beer (not unusual for a pub, but sick-making nonetheless). Corey immediately got told off for trying to light a cigarette indoors and was banished to the scruffy "beer garden", which was next to the car park but fenced off from it. In the venue, torn posters hung off the black painted walls, a couple of stray chairs and knocked-over beer glasses adorned the floor and, above all, it was freezing cold. But at least Mike, the long-suffering sound engineer, was present and ready to assist.

"Any idea how ticket sales are going?" he enquired, cheerfully.

This was something Ben had been trying to avoid thinking about. Having been so sadly let down by the local media, he felt pretty much that nobody even knew the show was happening. Online sales, he knew, were almost non-existent, but Sam had booked a local support act and maybe some of their friends would come. A couple of Ben's colleagues had promised to attend (he didn't really believe them). Rosie had tried, and failed, to interest some of her workmates. Had any been sold over the bar? Sam did a quick calculation and announced the grand total of advance tickets sold: thirteen. Ben hoped it wasn't an omen.

Corey found himself an old bar stool and unpacked his rucksack, which contained an array of effects pedals. Within moments, Ben felt relief sweeping over him. Corey's voice was intact, deep, emotional and resonant. His acoustic guitar, with the help of the pedals, produced an amazing array of sounds, echoing spookily round the empty room as Mike set the levels on the sound desk. Yes, he was going to lose his shirt. Yes, the lack of a crowd might be going to verge on embarrassing. But musically, it was going to be a hell of an evening.

Declaring himself satisfied with the sound, Corey said he was ready for dinner. He was unfamiliar with anything on the menu at the Light of Bengal, so Ben recommended that reliable staple Chicken Tikka Masala, which Corey consumed with relish. Then, to Ben's horror, he wandered out onto the pavement of Andover Road and casually lit up his little hash pipe. Surely, this, combined with the rich, unfamiliar food, was bound to induce onstage vomiting? Oh well, thought Ben, at least it'll be a talking point.

Back at The Station, the support band had arrived. This was a trio of local students called The Bookworms, with an acoustic act plainly modelled on Mumford and Sons. They may not have been particularly musically compatible with Corey, but they were competent and inoffensive. They also proudly announced that they had sold ten tickets to their friends. Things were looking up.

Rosie arrived and she and Ben opened the doors punctually at eight o'clock. They hadn't spoken for more than 24 hours and she was tense and irritable. Among early arrivals was a white-haired man with a faded Grams T-shirt and a Grams vinyl album under his arm, plainly brought for Corey to sign. His wife had a broken leg and requested a chair, which she plonked in front of the stage, her plastered limb resting on a monitor. Friends of the support band filtered in and stood along the walls, chatting. A few random, unidentified, balding middle-aged guys with beer bellies were there, too, and Ben recognized a couple of them from Americana shows in Basingstoke and Southsea. Robert arrived, incongruously still in his dark suit from work, and was talking to Rosie outside. Ben was grateful to Robert for agreeing to come and help out at an event he had no interest in, merely out of a sense of loyalty. All in all, it was a bittersweet feeling. Musically, it was going to be good, Ben was sure, but there was something downbeat, odd and uncomfortable about the atmosphere. It was soon to become a whole lot worse.

In the meantime, the support band had started playing their set, to intermittent applause. A small clutch of their friends was gathered in front the stage, watching them. To his amazement, Ben identified one of them as Carl, the pot dealer from Millbrook. Had he mentioned the gig to him? He was certain he hadn't, because all he'd wanted to do was get away from the tower block as fast as possible. Surely he couldn't be making a delivery to Corey? Anyway, he was probably mistaken, as one dreadlocked youth looked much the same as another.

About two songs in, the door opened and a tall figure in a tracksuit and a baseball cap, together with two other men, tried to barge past Rosie. Ben put out a hand to stop him and explain that there was an admission fee of £15. The man reacted badly.

"Get your fucking hands off me."

"I'm sorry, mate, but you have to pay to get in."

"I'm on the guest list."

"We haven't got a guest list."

"My cousin's in the support band, he said we didn't have to pay."

"I'm sorry, but I'm afraid you do."

A couple of people in the audience had already turned round and were making shushing noises. Ben was unsure what to do. This guy and his mates were aggressive and drunk, and he didn't want a row that could potentially develop into a fight. He couldn't expect Rosie to help out, Robert had disappeared into the other bar and Corey, who probably could have acted as a deterrent on account of his size, was lying low (and probably skinning up) in the upstairs broom cupboard which served as a dressing room. In the end, Ben made a decision.

"Well, you can come into now and we'll sort it out in the interval."

The guys lumbered in and went straight to the bar, where they chatted loudly. Ben wondered what the onstage cousin would be thinking of all this.

Rosie had some advice.

"Don't you know who that is?" she whispered.

"No. Should I?"

"That's Barry Mort."

"Who's Barry Mort?"

"I went to school with him. He's a bloody psychopath. He's done time for drug dealing, GBH, attempted murder, the lot."

Ben was vaguely aware of the extended Mort family, always in the Weekly News for some crime or other, usually violent. Mort, with its appropriately deadly connotations, was a local Hampshire name. This branch of the Morts was the nearest the country town had to a gang culture, with family members looking out for each other and intimidating potential witnesses to their various activities.

"Maybe he can get hold of some dope for Corey," thought Ben, glumly. But he was also genuinely scared. It was obvious that the Mort gang was already annoying others in the audience with their chatter. It would only take someone to say the wrong thing and it could kick off, ruining the evening. Not for the first time, Ben sincerely wished he'd never heard of Corey Zander, had never met that damn booking agent, and had never got himself into this scrape. He might come out of it with damage to more than just his pocket.

The Bookworms' set reached what they thought was a rousing climax and they left the stage to a smattering of applause. Sure enough, Barry Mort and his mates marched straight to the stage and started slapping the harmonica player on the back.

"Nice one Shane, cheers."

"Yeah, cheers, Baz."

Ben was now in a quandary. He could approach Barry and make an issue out of the payment, or he could hope that he'd go away when The Bookworms had packed up their gear. In view of what Rosie had told him, confrontation would be foolish, so Ben decided on caution. He could certainly have done with the admission fees, because the income so far had fallen woefully short of covering Corey's fee, but he could see no way that he could intimidate Barry into paying, nor, indeed, appeal to his better nature, as he didn't appear to have one. Staggering slightly, Mort and pals were helping The Bookworms to carry their gear out of the stage door, through which they eventually exited, doubtless to hang about smoking in the beer garden.

Robert, who had been working on his laptop at a corner table in the front bar, now entered the venue, looking thunderous and wildly out of place in his suit. He sat down behind the merchandise table. Ben had asked him to guard it while Corey was performing and while he looked after the door. Rosie, pleading a headache, had gone home in the interval, assuming that the Morts had gone and that it was unlikely there would be a sudden rush of customers that Ben wouldn't be able to cope with.

At 9:10, Corey Zander shuffled into the room. Not even the guy in the Grams T-shirt recognized him. As he tuned up his guitar and fiddled with his effects pedals, most of the assembled gaggle assumed he was a scruffy roadie, preparing the stage for the star. Ben was relieved to see that all The Bookworms' followers had disappeared into the beer garden too. He had too often experienced the scenario whereby the support band's fans ignore the headliner, talking all the way through his set. Thank God for the indoor smoking ban, thought Ben. That ought to keep them away.

This was where the evening looked up. There were about twenty people in the room, and Ben guessed most of them were familiar with Corey's back catalogue. It took a moment for them to realize that the show had started, because the random tuning up gradually metamorphosed into an echo maelstrom that abruptly became a song. As it settled into a groove, people gradually became aware that it was a radically rearranged version of "The Mountain", from the "Desert Grave" album. Utilizing a range of looping devices, Corey had found a way to make himself sound like a full band. It was fantastic.

As applause, whoops and whistles greeted each song, most of them entirely unfamiliar, Corey visibly relaxed. Towards the end of his 90-minute set, he started making the odd joke and telling a couple of anecdotes about the good old days, even asking if there were any requests. With the candles on the tables flickering away and the heating finally functioning, the atmosphere in the room was almost convivial. Sod the money, thought Ben, at least the evening has been a success.

"This will be my last song," said the gruff voice of Corey Zander. "Some of you may recognize it". Then, albeit at half the original speed and without the thunderous drums, the unmistakable riff of "Mad and Bad" rang out. People even started clapping along. And then it all went wrong.

Into the room crashed Barry Mort. He was on his own and he was very drunk. He was looking for something he'd left behind, but even he recognized the song.

"Yeah, you're fucking mad all right," he shouted. "You're fucking bad as well. You're shit."

People shifted uncomfortably. For a moment, Corey seemed to be going to try to ride it out, but Barry was unstoppable.

"Fuck you, you smelly old Yank. You're crap, and you know you are," he sang, pointing at the stage and trying to conduct the audience in the abusive football chant to the tune of the Village People.

That was enough for Corey. Stopping abruptly in mid-song, he stood up, carefully placed his guitar on its stand and advanced towards Barry Mort. Within seconds, Mort was up against the sticky wall with Corey's enormous hands round his throat. Mort may have been big, but Corey was bigger.

"Motherfucker," was the only word Corey used, "fucking motherfucker", as he maintained the pressure.

"Get off, let me go, I can't breathe," gasped Mort, as audience members, initially stunned, gathered round and tried to pull Corey off. As for Ben, he had indeed feared that there might be trouble, but he hadn't bargained for a full-on murder. Only ten minutes before, Corey had been singing a couple of murder ballads, now it seemed that death was genuinely on the agenda.

As Barry Mort slumped to the floor, Corey gradually released his grip, took a step back, landed a well aimed kick in Mort's testicles, pronounced, "You got what you deserved, motherfucker," and marched purposefully out of the door. Ben didn't know whether to follow him or attend to the wounded. In the end he ran over to the completely stunned Robert, to whom such a situation was unprecedented in his entire life, and asked him to see what had happened to Corey, while he kept an eye on Barry Mort.

Mort seemed okay. He recovered within a couple of minutes, pronounced, "That fucker ain't going know what's hit him," and headed for the beer garden in search of his gang.

"Please don't cause any more trouble," pleaded Ben.

"Fuck off, you cunt. I'm going to fucking kill him."

It could safely be said that the evening hadn't ended well. Wide-eyed audience members slunk for the exit, not even stopping off at the unmanned merchandise table. Of Corey there was no sign. Ben was in fear of his life, thinking he'd be in the Mort gang's firing line by association. Robert was nowhere to be seen either, so Ben helped Mike the sound engineer to clear up the stage. Corey's rucksack was still there, so they put the effects pedals in it. The guitar went back in its case and the Fender Twin amp Ben had hired from the local guitar shop was placed in a corner.

Daring to look out into the beer garden next to the dark car park, Ben couldn't see anyone about. He hoped that Mort and his mates hadn't gone after Corey, because those guys would probably be dab hands with baseball bats.

Unsure what to do, he then talked to Andy, the landlord. First, he collected the small amount of money that had accumulated, at the same time apologizing that things had gone so wrong.

"We should have had security on the door," admitted Andy, who, having pretty much seen everything over his years in the pub trade, didn't seem particularly bothered. "That Barry Mort has been banned from all Winchester pubs for years."

"I just didn't expect anything like that at all," said Ben. "Really, Sam shouldn't have booked that support band, then Mort wouldn't have been here in the first place."

"Oh well, no harm done really. Just put it down to experience," was Andy's philosophical conclusion.

Ben wasn't too impressed that Robert had obviously gone home, but he did understand how upsetting the incident must have been. There was nothing for it but to set out in search of Corey on his own. Given his reputation of simply "doing a runner", he could be anywhere. First, Ben walked to Oram's Arbour, a nearby park which was scattered with benches. Maybe Corey had hunkered down there? Then, just to check, he called Chilbolton Avenue, in case Corey had simply walked back there, but there was no answer. Diana took heavy-duty sleeping tablets, but Ben would have expected Robert to reply.

Winchester, late on Monday night, was dead. Ben walked along Jewry Street, past the Theatre Royal and the library, having a quick look in

St Peter's Church graveyard. The High Street was deserted apart from a few stray students on the way back to their residences. The Cathedral Grounds would have been a likely spot for Corey to crash out, but a passing security guard said he'd seen nothing unusual. Ben progressed past the fast-flowing River Itchen, momentarily wondering whether Corey might have stumbled into it, but he hadn't really been drunk and surely the incident, annoying as it was, hadn't been enough to induce thoughts of suicide? For a moment, Ben hesitated outside North Walls police station. Should he report Corey missing? That would presumably trigger a search operation, and Corey had "previous" in doing disappearing acts. Tired, fed up and pretty angry about how things had turned out, Ben set out to walk home to Weeke. On the way, he did a detour to the hospital, but there was no sign of Corey in Casualty. That was a relief. Now, as far as Ben was concerned, Corey could sleep outside in the cold, and sod him.

He felt crap in the morning.

"How did it go?" asked Rosie.

"I'll tell you later," replied Ben, grabbing a cereal bar and his work rucksack as he headed off on his usual walk to school, although things weren't "usual" at all. He arrived just in time for registration and assembly, which was being grimly conducted by Robert, who had at least changed into another suit. The theme was "love thy neighbour as thyself", and Ben felt Robert's eyes on him as he emphasized the importance of being kind to one's fellow humans. This was unfair. It wasn't as if Ben had planned any of this.

At break time, Ben knocked on Robert's door.

"I appreciate it was an unpleasant incident, Robert, but it was a bit unfair of you just abandon me to sort it all out."

"You make your bed, Ben, and you lie on it. Anyway, I was scared. Can't you see that, in my position, I can't get involved in any situation that could bring bad publicity on the school?"

Ben sighed. Robert was right, of course. He'd been an idiot to invite him in the first place. The music, the environment, the culture, everything about it had been alien to Robert, so how could he have expected support? Somehow, Ben got through the rest of the day, mainly by instructing the children to sit in silence and do written work, an approach that the children hated and that certainly would have earned him a reprimand from OFSTED.

Ben was sure that Corey would turn up. Apart from anything else, he needed to collect £500 from Ben, and then somehow get to Basingstoke for the next show. The plan had been for Ben to drive him there, but in view of what had happened, he now felt inclined simply to put him on a train.

The biggest worry was this: What if the Mort gang had actually found him? In that case there was a good chance that Corey was lying beaten up in some ditch, and that his tour wasn't going anywhere. But, on balance, Ben was confident that he would either be at the venue, in a coffee shop somewhere or, most likely, sleeping back at Chilbolton Avenue.

A phone call to Diana was disappointing. Corey hadn't returned. She'd been in all day but there had been no sign of him. Ben's next stop would have to be The Station. The gear would have had to be retrieved anyway and Corey would probably have headed there to collect it. Why didn't the idiot have a mobile phone? For the rest of the tour, Ben would recommend him to buy a pay-as-you-go phone to avoid losing touch with the other hapless promoters.

As he expected, The Station was deserted. There were just a couple of cars in the large car park. On the ground, Ben spotted an empty Coke bottle and a couple of discarded kebab containers. A good upbringing and years of telling children never to leave litter meant Ben was one of those people who always pick up rubbish. In the far corner of the car park was the large refuse container, used by the venue to dispose of its garbage. As he opened the lid, Ben noticed a trail of ketchup leaking out from behind it.

Disgusting. Bending down to see if he could do anything about clearing it up, Ben suddenly choked and with a shiver of shock, realized that he was living a cliché: yes, it wasn't ketchup, it was blood. Wedged behind the bin, invisible to anyone not walking up and examining it, was a large bundle of grey clothes. As Ben moved the wheeled container forward, he saw the truth: it wasn't a bundle of old clothes, it was Corey Zander.

Breathless, Ben didn't, for a moment, panic. He assumed Corey must have crawled behind there to sleep, having returned late at night to find The Station locked. He'd taken the bourbon with him so had most likely been on a bender. Released from where the bin had held him against the wall, Corey was now lying on his back. Copying what he'd seen in a thousand TV crime shows, Ben, when there was no reply to his request to wake up, slapped the bewhiskered face a couple of times. Nothing. Christ, surely he wasn't dead? Ben listened for a breath. Nothing. It was just weeks since Ben had attended a First Aid course at the River Park Leisure Centre, so his instinct kicked in. He started pumping Corey's chest. "Sing 'Staying Alive' as you do it, to get the correct rhythm", he had been taught. So there he was, a surreal picture in a sordid litter-strewn car park, fruitlessly pressing up and down on a strange American's chest while singing aloud a Bee Gees song. Once again, nothing. Ben stood up and looked at his hands. From where he had been trying to cradle Corey's head, they were covered with blood. There was no way around it. Corey was dead.

Chapter 5

At North Walls police station, Tuesday afternoons were normally quiet. Apart from the motorway guys, who often had traffic accidents on the M3 to deal with, there was little to do apart from catch up on paperwork. Maybe a minor domestic dispute in Highcliffe would need to be sorted out, or a shoplifter would be apprehended in the Brooks shopping centre. So, despite himself, Detective Chief Inspector Robin Bird actually felt a frisson of excitement when he was told that a body had been found. Most likely it would be a homeless alcoholic, but who knows, maybe it could be a juicy murder? In this provincial backwater, murder was more or less unknown. A few years earlier, a lady in Weeke had been strangled by a spurned lover, and there was the still unsolved murder of a pensioner in Brambridge, but generally, the sort of case normally dealt with by Bird and his team tended to be a lot more mundane.

Taking his colleague DI Adrian Jackson with him, and cursing the clogged up rush-hour one-way system, Bird had to switch on the siren to carve his way through. Uniform and medics were already on the scene, as Ben had called 999 the second he realized that Corey was dead. Bird called ahead to remind the medics not to move the body in case, just in case - he almost hoped - it was a murder case.

Bird and Jackson arrived at The Station to find a pretty dismal scene. A cluster of people were gathered round behind a taped-off area containing a large, scruffy figure on the ground. The refuse bin had been moved out of the way by someone. The congealed "ketchup" emanated from the back of the body's head, so it was immediately clear that a pathologist would have to be called. Attempting to take charge and ascertain the background, Bird asked for any information anyone might have.

"Does anyone know who this is?"

"I do."

It was a pale-faced, nervous, frightened-looking young man who replied.

He was respectably dressed but his jacket and hands seemed to be bloodstained, which, Bird thought, needed further investigation.

"Who are you?"

"I'm Ben Walker. I know who this guy is. He's Corey Zander."

"Is he local?"

"No, not at all. He's American." This seemed unexpectedly exotic.

"How do you know him?"

"He played a show here last night. I promoted it. There was a bit of trouble during the evening, but I don't know if it's connected. Corey ran off but maybe he came back here in the night and something happened."

"And what's your explanation for the blood that's on you?"

"I'm the one who found him. I got the blood on me as I tried to revive him."

"Okay, well, make sure you stay around." Bird turned to his colleague. "It could have been an accident, but for now, we'll view it as a suspicious death. We'll wait to see what the pathologist says. Maybe that'll help make things clearer."

In the meantime, Bird and Jackson set about looking at the body as far as they could without disturbing it. Then, making sure no one stepped beyond the tape and contaminated the area, they questioned Andy the landlord and his assistant Sam, both of whom had emerged from the pub and were standing around, looking shell-shocked. Neither of them could add anything to clarify the picture. The guy had played a gig the night before, and now, here he was, dead in the car park. It made little sense.

Jackson was speaking to DCI Bird. "Well, he looks like he's in his fifties, he's very overweight and he doesn't look too healthy. I'd guess he probably had a heart attack and hit his head on something as he fell, maybe that rubbish bin."

He called Ben over. “Had this guy been drinking? Did he do drugs?”

As he detailed the possibilities, Ben felt he’d landed in some rock ‘n’ roll movie that he wished he’d never seen.

“Well, he had a history of drug misuse, but he quit hard drugs many years ago. He may have had some dope, and he had whisky on him, because I bought it for him. But he was quite sober when I last saw him. He put on a great show.”

The pathologist who turned up was a lady, Misha Patel. All in all, it felt like a scene from “Midsomer Murders”, as she examined the body in the gathering dusk. The medics stood in the corner with nothing to do. Andy, Sam and Ben had retreated into the pub and Andy’s wife Carol was making tea for everyone. Bird and Jackson looked at their watches and waited to hear what Ms Patel would say. One way, they could ask for the body to be removed, do some paperwork for next of kin and move on. The other way, they could expect to be embarking on a major investigation.

Patel stood up.

“What do you think?”

“Well, as far as I can tell from a quick examination, the cause of death is a massive blow to the back of the head with a large, rough-edged instrument.”

“Could he have stumbled and hit himself on something?”

“Unlikely. Even if he was very drunk, he would most likely have stumbled forwards and this bin is made of plastic and hasn’t got any rough edges. Besides, how did he end up behind it? Did he crawl there with a gaping hole in his head?”

Bird nodded. “It looks like someone has tried to hide the body.”

“That’s what it looks like, yes.”

“So it’s looking like murder.” Bird was thinking aloud, rather than asking.

"Of course, I can't be specific until after the post-mortem, but my unofficial first impression is that, yes, that is the most likely explanation."

Bird and Jackson took charge. Bird called the Control Room and requested a murder squad to be put in place. Then, the entire building, beer garden and car park were sealed off with incident tape. There would be no gig at the Station tonight. Andy was horrified; business was crap enough as it was, without having to close the venue to customers. A baffled looking indie band from London, arriving in their Sprinter van, were turned away with no more explanation than, "Sorry, this is now a crime scene". This would make a good story for the NME.

The medics were put in charge of carefully gathering up the body and transporting it to somewhere where the clothes could be removed and prepared for forensic examination. A team of officers from North Walls, supplemented with a few from Eastleigh, were brought in to conduct an intensive search of the scene. If there was any evidence, it was going to be there in the car park. The items they turned up were a fascinating collection, although none of obvious relevance. There were thousands of cigarette ends, plus beer bottle caps, broken guitar strings, the remains of a capo, a splintered drumstick and, oh dear, a used condom, presumably from some punters who couldn't wait to get home and had used the car park instead.

In the end, the evidence was in the obvious place. Two officers from the search team, brought in from the Hampshire Police Support HQ in Netley, had been given the unenviable task of sorting through the rubbish bin. Halfway down, amongst the dirty paper plates, the beer cans, the crisp and cigarette packets and the plastic bags and, strangely, a half-full bottle of Bourbon, they found the murder weapon. It was a large, battered brick and it had a very clear bloodstain on one side of it. The officer who found it was wearing latex gloves, so didn't contaminate it too much as he held it triumphantly aloft.

"Sir, look at this."

Whoever had killed Corey Zander hadn't made much of an effort to hide the weapon; it seemed to have been simply tossed into the bin. Any fingerprints on the lid handle would be interesting, thought Bird, as he ushered everyone away and ordered the whole car park to be designated as a major crime scene. Andy the landlord, having been watching through the window, came out to add his contribution.

"That's the brick we use to prop open the stage door. It's normally just lying around in the car park."

It's going to be a straightforward case, thought Bird. No hidden gun, no knife stolen from a kitchen, not even an old-fashioned baseball bat. Corey's killer had quite obviously simply picked up the nearest blunt object and thumped him when it. All they had to do was find someone with motive and opportunity and that would be that. But who might that someone be? It was pretty obvious who the main candidate was. One person was standing right there with blood, literally, on his hands. It had to be that young promoter. There was, at the very least, reasonable suspicion.

It was true that Ben, in his stunned condition, hadn't even got round to washing. Why should he have? The last thing he would have considered would be that he could be a suspect. He'd spent half the night searching for Corey. He actually sort of liked him. And what conceivable motive might he have had for killing him? Not that he was thinking about any of these things right now. He was just standing around, crushed.

"Are we going to arrest Ben Walker?" Bird asked Jackson.

"Well, you can't say he doesn't look suspicious."

"We'll certainly have to bring him in for questioning."

When he was asked to accompany the officers to the police station, the words penetrated Ben's brain through a mist of incomprehension. Two days ago, he'd been a conventional schoolteacher in the process of planning his wedding. Now he was being taken in for interrogation about a murder. It was beyond belief.

As Ben got into a police van, Bird discussed the next steps with Jackson. The brick was carefully bagged up and taken, along with all the other debris, to North Walls. Corey's body was in the process of being removed. The crime scene remained sealed off and a little convoy of police vehicles snaked back round the one-way system, with Ben in the leading van.

At North Walls, Ben was given permission to make a phone call. Unsurprisingly, Rosie was by turns incredulous, speechless, mortified and eventually hysterical. How could something like this happen to a family like theirs? Whatever had Ben got himself into? She eventually agreed to contact Robert and Diana, who would surely have access to good lawyers.

While preparing to question Ben, DCI Bird had an important thought: What about next of kin? Having no clue as to how to contact anyone, he asked Ben.

"According to my researches, Corey has parents in Oklahoma and a daughter in Texas. But I don't know any more that that."

"Is there any way of contacting them?"

"Well, I have the phone number of his agent. He might be able to help."

He was able to give Bird the number, which was stored on his mobile phone. Bird then gave Glenn Wallis probably the worst phone call of his life. His well-meaning plan of arranging for Corey Zander to tour Europe had crashed to the ground in the most final and spectacular manner imaginable. He promised to try and find a way to contact Corey's family.

"It's the Curse of Zander," said Glenn.

"What?" Bird was in no mood for a loony distracting him from the business in hand.

"Oh, it's just a bit of nonsense. Guys in the industry used to joke that Zander was cursed. He was a bit of an oddball, his father was an alcoholic, he was a junkie and his wife died."

"Yeah, well, the Curse has really kicked in now," replied Bird, grimly.

Glenn had set up the entire tour by e-mail, directly through Corey himself. He started by sending an e-mail to that address, in the hope that Corey's daughter would maybe look at his computer. He rang a couple of friends in Austin and asked them to try and get hold of a number for Lucy. He also posted a message on Corey's Facebook page, asking anyone who knew Corey or Lucy to contact him urgently. And finally, he put a similar request on his own Twitter feed.

Ben received a cup of tea before being led to an interview room, where DCI Bird and DS Jackson awaited him. Robert had engaged a lawyer called Maria Weston to represent him.

"For the purpose of the tape ..." Ben was amazed that the police actually did still use audiocassettes. They'd been phased out as an educational tool a decade ago. In a daze, he heard Bird's voice.

"In our opinion, Mr Walker, there is enough evidence for you to be cautioned and charged. You will be appearing in court in the morning for a preliminary hearing, and in the meantime you'll be remanded in custody."

Ben took a deep breath and somehow retained his presence of mind.

"I will of course be denying the charge. Other than that, I have no comment."

At ten o'clock the next morning, after an uncomfortable and fretful night in the cells, he was taken to court for one of those brief "confirming name and address" hearings. Ben's first priority would be to ask his lawyer to get him released, as, even if they thought he had murdered Corey Zander, he surely wasn't a danger to others. In court, he noticed a reporter from the Weekly News scribbling away in shorthand. He could already picture the next edition's headline: Local Teacher On Murder Charge.

....

Lucy Cruz was in the process of helping to set up an exhibition of her photographs at the Yard Dog Gallery on South Congress in Austin when the gallery owner approached her. She'd seen a Facebook public entry scrolling down the side of her screen. "If anyone in Austin knows Lucy Cruz, could you ask her to call this number urgently". Lucy used the gallery's phone to call Glenn Wallis, who had posted the message. She knew he was her father's UK agent, so the news had to be something to do with Corey.

"Hey, Glenn, what's up?"

"Lucy, I have some bad news. It's about your father."

Lucy swallowed, but somehow she wasn't altogether surprised to receive a call. He'd had a triple heart bypass the year before, so she feared the worst.

"He's had a heart attack?"

"No, he's had some kind of accident. We don't really understand what happened."

"Is he okay?"

"I don't know how to tell you... apparently, he's dead."

For a few moments, Lucy couldn't bring herself to speak. She had had her doubts about the wisdom of Corey's European adventure all along, but he'd argued the "nothing ventured, nothing gained" approach. At this stage in his career, what was there to lose? It might even be fun. Lucy had even considered accompanying him as tour manager, until they looked at the prices of transatlantic flights. Maybe, if she'd been with him, this accident, or whatever it was, could have been avoided. She instantly felt guilt for not having been with him.

"I'll have to come over."

"I think that would be good. Let me know when you have your flight details and I'll get someone to meet you at the airport."

"Where is he?"

"He's in a town called Winchester, near London."

"What kind of accident was it? A crash on the highway?"

"No, he received a head injury but no one knows how."

Lucy and her father had lived together for over 20 years in a small house at the back of Home Slice Pizza, south of the Colorado River in Austin. In an unofficial capacity, Lucy had effectively been his manager, getting him solo gigs at various venues across Texas and neighbouring states. For the last couple of years, she'd even been driving him around. His driving felony had been a marginal thing, really, just a couple of beers that an audience member had bought him, but Texas's draconian traffic laws had meant a lengthy ban.

Lucy had been eight when she and Corey made the move to Texas. He'd already had two stabs at the mainstream music industry and correctly assumed that Austin would be an ideal environment to "settle down". With a history of drug abuse, Corey needed to be somewhere where he could be sure of regular work as a solo artist, and where his daughter could be brought up in a liberal atmosphere. Surrounded by supportive musicians, he entered a world of jam sessions, studio work and creative conversation, a long way from the conservative world of Oklahoma. Unsurprisingly, Lucy displayed both musical and artistic talent at school, eventually studying fine art at the University of Texas. Her photography and painting, often inspired by her Choctaw heritage, could be seen on album covers, in coffee table books and in galleries throughout the state.

Lucy inherited the talents and looks of her parents. She was very beautiful, in an "alternative" style, wafting round the cultural city in long flowing dresses, every bit the modern-day hippie. Both she and Corey had occasional relationships, but the father-daughter bond remained strong. Lucy looked out for her dad. His history meant that he could be volatile and his health needed keeping an eye on. Apart from his daily marijuana, he had completely given up using any drugs, and alcohol was restricted to the occasional margarita or the odd Lone Star beer. It was rare for him to have an outburst of rage, but it happened if he was severely provoked. Lucy blamed the drug abuse of his youth for "messing with his brain" and, like many offspring of alcoholic or drug addicted parents, she determinedly rejected both those vices. Lucy was also a vegetarian and a keep fit enthusiast, jogging daily in Zilker Park and regularly doing yoga and Pilates.

In this, she was also rejecting her father's lifestyle. His heart attack had taken place two years before, packing up after a gig in San Antonio. He'd been rushed to hospital and saved, after a frantic search of a shoe box at the bottom of his bedroom wardrobe by Lucy had revealed enough cash to assure the hospital he could pay for the operation – he wasn't insured, of course. He had a couple of stents inserted, and proceeded to carry on with exactly his old lifestyle. He'd love to go to IHOP for breakfast, a huge stack of pancakes with bacon. Lunch would be a short walk to the pizza joint and evenings would often entail a trip to Wendy's for a burger with plenty of salt. Lucy tried and tried to reform his lifestyle, but to no avail. His youth in the Lance-A-Lot chain, with its daily freebies, was to blame, of that Lucy was sure. Sport was out of the question. Corey's routine would be to walk to his pickup, drive to the gig, sit on a stool as he played, and drive home again. That's why Lucy, while obviously distraught, wasn't completely surprised by the news from England. In a way, she'd been fearing it for a while.

"Is there anyone else I should contact?" asked Glenn. "Are his parents still alive?"

Both Aileen and Lance had passed away in the last few years. Lance had gone first, the stress of the job having helped to induce a stroke. People said Aileen had died of a broken heart, and in a sense that was true. She'd gradually gone downhill but the official cause of death had been some form of cancer. She, too, had over-indulged in the greasy food, but Lance's sons had inherited the business and it continued to thrive.

Lucy was comforted by Ramona Cullis, her friend and duty manager at Yard Dog that day. Lucy headed straight home to investigate flights and Ramona couldn't resist going online to break the news on Facebook and Twitter. Within hours, the whole of Austin, and indeed the whole worldwide Americana community was digesting the tragic news: Corey Zander was dead, circumstances unknown. Sites like No Depression, Maverick and Americana-UK.com posted updates. A hastily created Facebook tribute page received hundreds of hits, with Austin luminaries such as Ian McLagan, Slaid Cleaves and Bob Schneider posting messages of sympathy.

For once, money was not the top issue for Lucy as she searched for flights. Frugality had been a way of life for her and her dad for decades, but the priority today was speed. She found a route, leaving the following morning, which started at Austin's Bergstrom airport, connected in Chicago and Paris and terminated at Southampton airport, which Glenn had said was the closest to Winchester. Lucy clicked to book, inserted her credit card details and started to pack.

....

In Winchester, one forensics team was minutely examining the car park at The Station, while another was analysing Corey Zander's clothes. Either of these could produce vital clues as to the identity of Corey's killer, and gradually, what they found was being filtered back to Robin Bird at North Walls. In the meantime, DS Jackson and a couple of other officers were assigned to track down every person who had been present at the gig and interview each of them. It wasn't a terribly difficult task, as so few people had been there. Still on the little table by the door was the paperwork: the Bookworms' list of people they'd sold to, the printouts of the online sales and the mailing list where Ben had asked "walk-up" guests to leave their details so he could add them to a mailing list and inform them about – ha, ha – future gigs.

First, Jackson interviewed Andy and Sam from The Station in more detail. Both of them had been working the bar that evening, so both were well informed.

"What about this incident with the Mort gang?"

"Well, we'd never have let Barry Mort in under normal circumstances, but he took us by surprise. He isn't interested in music, but it turns out his cousin was in the support band and he invited him along. Ben Walker tried to stop him getting in without paying, but he just barged past."

"What happened to Mort?"

"He was causing trouble at the gig and Corey Zander attacked him. I don't know where he went after that, he and his mates all just ran away."

Mort would have to be paid a visit very soon, thought Jackson.

"We have reason to believe that Ben Walker might be involved in all this. Was he acting normally?"

"I don't know what normal is to him, he'd never hired the place before. But he was definitely nervous, mainly because he was going to lose a lot of money on the night. Plus he was freaked when Barry Mort and his mates showed up."

Sam intervened, then hesitated. "Also..., oh, it's not important."

"What's not important?"

"Well, he was telling me that Corey sent him to Southampton to buy drugs. He was trying to laugh about it, but I think he was nervous. He said he had to deal with some dodgy characters there."

"Interesting." Jackson made a note.

At the same time, a couple of officers were up at Peter Symonds College, where the principal had managed to gather the Bookworms plus all their friends who had attended. They genuinely seemed to have nothing to add, apart from pointing out that they hadn't been paid. All agreed that the Bookworms had simply played their set and left, spending the next hour smoking in the beer garden. Nobody had anything negative to say about Barry Mort and his friends; yes, they'd had a bit to drink, but they'd helped them take their gear out to their car. They didn't know anything about them barging in without paying. They hadn't put them on the guest list because they didn't have one and anyway they'd had no idea they were coming.

Robin Bird rang Rosie at work. Despite the madness, she'd gone in as usual, but wasn't concentrating. She told the truth, which was that she'd stayed for a while but gone home early with a headache. She berated Bird with the ridiculousness of arresting her fiancé, who would never hurt anyone in a million years. Bird then caught Robert Leighton on the phone in his lunch break at school. He'd heard from Rosie about the arrest and was also amazed and angry that one of his loyal staff was under suspicion. He'd had to draft in a supply teacher and it was all most inconvenient.

"Did you witness the incident when Barry Mort was attacked by Zander?"

"I saw it, yes, but I didn't want to get involved, so I left immediately."

"Where did you go?"

"I went home. I hadn't enjoyed the music anyway, I was only there because Ben wanted me to come."

"You can't shed any light on all this?"

"I'm afraid I can't, but I'll tell you one thing. There's no chance that Ben would ever be involved in violence and I can't understand why you've arrested him. I'm sure it must have all been some kind of accident."

Robert went on to ask Bird if there was any way that he could exert influence to keep the details of the arrest out of the papers. Bird replied that this was beyond his powers, and when Robert got home that evening and switched on the TV, Sally Taylor of South Today was just reading the main headline: "An American rock star has been killed in a shock incident in England's ancient capital. A local primary teacher has been arrested". The report was accompanied by a mug shot of Ben and, oh God, some footage of parents picking up their children from St John's School, the youngsters' faces pixelated out. This was beyond ridiculous.

Back at the venue, Jackson was just leaving when he remembered a final question for Sam the barman.

"I know what I was going to ask. You said Ben was set to lose a lot of money. Do you know exactly how much?"

Sam started doing some sums on his iPhone's calculator.

"Okay, well, Corey's fee was £500. Ben had to pay £60 for the sound engineer and £100 to hire the room. Plus I know he bought him dinner and drove to Heathrow and back. So that's probably about 700 quid in all. The support band brought 10 people, but the tickets were half-price. We sold 13 advance tickets at £15 each, and four people paid on the door, so that's a total income of..." He tapped... "£330". He tapped again. "So he was in a hole to the tune of £370. That's quite a lot for a young teacher."

"Would it be enough to kill for, though?" mused Jackson, as he thanked Sam and drove back down to North Walls to report his findings to Bird. Bird himself had received a wealth of interesting news from the forensics teams and was preparing to interview Ben Walker again. Jackson agreed, despite the fact that he would rather have gone home, to sit in on the session.

"Mr Walker, we've now looked into this case in some detail, and we have good reason to believe that you killed Corey Zander on Monday evening."

"That's crazy. You're basing this on the fact that I had blood on my hands. It's obvious that the blood came from when I was holding his head and trying to resuscitate him. Do you honestly think I got covered with blood while killing him the night before and hadn't washed since?"

"My theory is this. You're an educated man. You know as well as I do that you can scrub as much as you like but our forensics guys will still find traces of blood under your fingernails even when they seem clean. That man was cold, he'd obviously been dead for hours. What was the point of trying to resuscitate him? I know exactly what you were up to. You purposely got blood on your hands to confuse the issue."

Ben shook its head. Surely this was the most far-fetched conspiracy theory he had ever heard of.

"Listen, I quite liked Corey. I'd just found him and my natural instinct was to try and revive him. He walked out of that room and I didn't see him again until I found him behind that container. What possible reason would I have to kill him, even if I was capable of killing anyone?"

"Ah," Bird smiled, as everything continued to fall into place in his mind. "I don't believe it was premeditated. I think it just happened. Here's what I think. You followed him out into the car park and tried to calm him down. He was in a rage because of what Barry Mort had done to him. He blamed you for getting him such a bad gig, where he'd been humiliated."

"No..."

"Yes. That made you angry too. You'd lost £370 on the gig and you told him so. You told him he should be grateful that you'd given him the opportunity. You argued, and this is the bit that is missing. Maybe he turned his back on you and you picked up the brick and hit him. Or maybe you just pushed him and he fell and hit his head on it."

"I couldn't push Corey Zander over if I tried. And I wouldn't want to anyway. We didn't argue and I certainly didn't kill him. You need to be investigating Barry Mort, not me. You have absolutely no evidence against me, because there isn't any."

"Ah, but I think you'll find we have." Bird was smiling again. He reached into a folder and pulled out a small polythene evidence bag. "Do you recognize this?"

Ben looked at the item in the bag. It was a small promotional button badge, about two inches across. Emblazoned on it, in green on black, was The Grams' logo. Ben had seen that Corey was wearing it on his jacket, a delightful piece of nostalgia to bring back memories of the 80s.

"Yes, of course. Corey was wearing it."

"You remember that we fingerprinted you when we took you into custody yesterday? Well, there's a print on that badge that exactly matches yours. Do you have a comment?"

It was so obvious, that Ben didn't hesitate.

"Of course my fingerprint is on it. He was wearing it on his chest and I was pumping his chest to try and resuscitate him. It's a pretty straightforward explanation."

"It may be straightforward in your version of events. It's straightforward in my version too. That fingerprint comes from when you were fighting and you pushed him."

Ben couldn't think of anything else to say. He turned to his solicitor.

"What can I do?"

Jackson intervened. "You see, Mr Walker, we have the impression that you're not quite the respectable citizen you paint yourself as. We've been told by a reliable source that you were hanging around in dodgy parts of Southampton trying to purchase drugs for your American so-called 'friend'."

"And you admitted yourself that you supplied him with whiskey," added Bird. "Surely that wasn't going to improve his performance?"

The lawyer, Mrs Weston, looked at from the notes. "I'm tempted to say, 'It'll never stand up in a court of law'," was her comment. The evidence is flimsy, largely irrelevant and circumstantial and it's unlikely a jury would be convinced by any of it. There's absolutely no reason for you to hold my client in custody, so I'm requesting bail."

"I'm afraid that's not possible," responded Bird. "That's not the only piece of evidence we have."

His hands returned to the folder and drew out a colour photograph. It showed something green and it was hard to see at first what it was.

"Do you know what this is?"

"I'm not sure."

"I'll tell you. It's the handle of the refuse container in the car park of the station. Can you explain why your fingerprints are on here too?"

For a second, Ben slumped. He'd always had a bit of a "victim complex". Why had he always come last in school sports? Why had his results always just been average? Why had he never been promoted? Why was Robert always telling him off? It felt as if someone had it in for him, but why? All his intentions had been good, but everything had gone wrong. This policeman seemed determined to stitch him up, but why? Then he remembered.

"Yes... yes, I can explain. I found some rubbish on the floor of the car park and I opened the bin to put it in."

Bird sighed and looked quizzically at the prisoner. "So, there's the dead body of someone you know in the car park, and all you can think about is clearing up litter? You're going to have to do better than that, Mr Walker."

Chapter 6

Bird did indeed have a reason to try and secure a conviction against Ben, and it was a simple one. Statistics were important in modern policing. Clear-up rates were published nationally and individual officers were measured on successful prosecutions. A conviction in a murder case like this would look fantastic on his curriculum vitae and it was very rare for such an opportunity to arise in sleepy Winchester. But the more he thought about it, the greater his doubts became. Was he really so convinced of Ben's guilt? Just because he seemed a bit of a middle class twit, and was seemingly involved in the business end of quite a seedy industry, it didn't necessarily mean he was a murderer, Bird was forced to acknowledge to himself. Further forensic results put fibres from Ben's duffle coat on Corey Zander's jacket, but that also could be explained as having happened during the resuscitation attempt.

As it stood, there was definitely a case to answer, but Bird could already hear how the judge would instruct the jury: "If you have the slightest doubt about the guilt of the defendant, you must return a verdict of Not Guilty". This case was not as open and shut as he had initially dared to hope, and the wrath of the media would land on his head if thousands of pounds were spent on a failed prosecution. The press loved to lay into the obvious suspect, but would be equally merciless on the police if the obvious suspect turned out to be innocent. Ben Walker seemed so crushed that Bird couldn't imagine him absconding, so, after discussion with colleagues and Maria Weston, Bird agreed to allow bail. Robert and Diana came up with the surety and, after a second night in the cells, Ben was released on Thursday morning.

"I hope you realize that this doesn't mean you're no longer under suspicion," Bird emphasized to Ben.

Walking along City Road and into Andover Road, past the Albion, where Corey had unsuccessfully tried to score drugs, and the Light of Bengal, where they had dined only days before, Ben hardly recognized the world. Everything was normal, the commuters heading to the station, the students strolling up towards Peter Symonds College, but his world could never be the same. The consequences of getting into trouble in a small town were about to kick in, and he knew it.

As he turned the corner into Taplings Road, he noticed a couple of neighbours talking. As they saw him, they turned away to avoid having to say Good Morning. He obviously couldn't go in to school, so he decided to stay in the flat and phone the various people he needed to contact. He started by calling Rosie at work at Pooles. She expressed relief at his release, but explained, in a low voice, that she couldn't talk at the moment because people were giving her strange looks.

He then tried Robert at school. It was morning break and Robert had some time to talk, but his response wasn't the sympathetic one Ben had foolishly hoped for. There was a list as long as his arm of reasons why this incident had been disastrous. He'd had to find thousands of pounds to bail Ben out. Diana was on the verge of a nervous breakdown, being spurned by all her influential friends. Parents were threatening to take their children away from the school, not wishing them to be associated with a teacher involved in a sordid murder case. He was going to have to spend a fortune on supply teachers. The governors had convened a special meeting for this evening with a single item on the agenda: the suspension of Ben Walker.

"Suspension?" Ben was feeling dizzy. "Why should I be suspended when I haven't done anything wrong?"

"Whether you've done anything wrong is a matter of opinion. I don't believe you're a murderer but I do believe you were irresponsible, as a teacher, to get involved in something like this. If we're not careful it'll ruin the reputation of the school and I'll be implicated by association. I'm sorry, I can't be seen to support you in public. I only hope Rosie will."

It was like being diagnosed with a terminal illness. This would have been an ideal moment to consult a close and trusted friend, but Ben didn't have any. He'd lost touch with most of his old uni friends and he and Rosie only socialized with work colleagues, with whom their relationships were cordial but superficial. Ben's entire existence had been turned to jelly. If he wasn't careful, he'd drown. He had to try to force himself to concentrate on practicalities, on getting things done, otherwise panic would turn to inertia. Already his instinct was simply to go to bed, pull the covers over his head and hope that he'd wake up in a parallel world where everything was all right. He rang Glenn Wallis, who had some news.

"I've managed to contact Lucy Cruz, Corey's daughter, and she's already on her way. She seems to be Corey's only surviving relative. I've been busy contacting all the other promoters on the tour, telling them they'll have to cancel their shows. It hasn't been fun."

"Well, I guess there's one practical thing I can do," concluded Ben. "If you tell me when she is arriving, I can collect Lucy from the airport."

"She's coming FlyBe from Paris, arriving at 6.40 on Saturday morning."

Ben was almost expecting that Rosie would join her father in berating him for his stupidity, but when she came in from work, she embraced and comforted him with kind words. Her show of support made him release, in the form of tears, all the emotion that had been building up: Terror, rage at the injustice of it all, fear and uncertainty about the future. He was so grateful at being shown some affection at last.

"Ben, I know there is absolutely no way that you could have done such a thing. There's nothing to be gained by going back over the past, so let's just concentrate on the future and clearing your name."

Entwined on the sofa, with little to say but much to think about, the pair finally managed to sleep.

....

Back at the police station, Bird had convened a small meeting to sum up the situation. The consensus was that he was right to have doubts about Ben's guilt.

"The fact is," pointed out Jackson, "that the fingerprint on the badge could easily have come from Walker pressing on his chest. He just doesn't seem the type. What do the rest of you think?"

Barbara Sellers, a station sergeant, agreed. "It's the same with the refuse bin handle. Okay, it's unlikely that he would be picking up litter, but it's perfectly possible. There are scores of people's fingerprints all over it and whoever put the brick in there could have been any one of them."

"And the fibres," admitted Bird, "they could also have come, as he said, from the resuscitation attempt. Also, the two of them had been together for days. You know what those Americans are like, maybe he gave him a bear hug to thank him for getting the dope."

Everyone laughed. "As for the dope," added Barbara, "strictly speaking, what he did was illegal, but it's another matter altogether. It doesn't make him a killer."

"I wouldn't give much for his chances of keeping his job, though."

....

It was Friday morning again, and a lot had changed in the week since Ben had checked out the entertainments page in the Weekly News. This time, his walk to the Co-op was a lot less jaunty. He kept his head bowed as he handed over the 95p. This time, he didn't need to search through the pages, as his own face stared out from the front page in full colour. Taking its cue from South Today, the Weekly News had also superimposed it over a photo of St John's School and a close-up of the board outside it saying "Headteacher: Dr Robert Leighton". The News had gone to press the night before and as far as it was concerned, Ben was still in custody. Ben noted that Derek White had put a lot more effort into this news item then he had into plugging his gig.

CAR PARK MURDER – TEACHER HELD

> Police are holding Winchester primary teacher Ben Walker in custody, charged with killing a man, believed to be American musician Corey Zander, in the car park of The Station venue in the city. It is understood that the ex-rocker was bludgeoned to death after his show last Monday, allegedly connected to an argument about money. Detective Chief Inspector Robin Bird, leading the enquiry, said that there were still many avenues of investigation to explore and that the arrest did not mean that they were not looking for anyone else in connection with the case. Walker has been a class teacher at St John's Primary School for several years. Head teacher Robert Leighton was unavailable for comment. Worried parents gathered at the school gates to discuss the shocking events. Sharon Brown (36) commented, "I can't believe it. We always thought Mr Walker was a nice man and a good teacher and now he turns out to be a murderer. I'll certainly be taking my children out of school if he ever returns."

Back at the flat, the postman was waiting at the door. A Recorded Delivery envelope, which Ben had to sign for, contained a formal letter from Hampshire County Council, confirming his suspension on full pay. That was that, then. Even if he managed to clear his name, life in Winchester could scarcely be bearable again. He didn't know what to do with himself. He could hardly walk down to the school and plead his case with Robert. He couldn't embarrass Rosie by visiting her in her lunch break. He felt like storming back into the police station and telling them to pull themselves together and stop being so ridiculous. In the end, he spent time flicking through internet pages on his laptop. All the news items and tributes were peppered with "allegedlys" and "it is believeds". Reporters were being careful to make veiled accusations but not make themselves liable to legal action if he was innocent. Just as well, because in his current mood, he'd have sued every one of them.

In the afternoon, Ben rang Diana and went round to Chilbolton Avenue for tea. She tried hard, she really did. The humiliation and the scorn at the hands of her posh friends must have been hard to bear, but Robert's claim that she was close to a breakdown had been an exaggeration. She was clear in her mind that Ben wouldn't have been involved, even though the circumstances and the milieu in which all this had occurred were a total mystery to her. This sort of thing certainly didn't go on in the Waynflete Singers or at the Chesil Theatre. Ben told her the entire story in detail.

"Okay, we know you didn't do it," said Diana, "so who did?"

"It's obvious who did it, that's why I can't understand why they went for me. It was Barry Mort."

"But are you sure?"

"Who else would have wanted to harm Corey? Mort was drunk, he has a record of violence and he was provoked. He's a thug."

"How can you prove it?"

"That's not my job, that's up to the police. But I'm going to get my lawyer to find out why they aren't pursuing that line of enquiry."

....

As it happened, minds at North Walls were finally turning in that direction too. With the team already having doubts, some information had come in that was to take the focus off Ben as a suspect.

The CCTV evidence had been retrieved, edited and delivered to Bird. In an initiative funded by the shops and businesses of Winchester, a comprehensive CCTV network covered the entire city centre. Like many UK cities, Winchester was populated at weekend evenings by crowds of students and other youngsters, mixed with off-duty soldiers from the barracks on the outskirts. There was always trouble in the form of scuffles, fights, general drunkenness and vomiting, even the odd sexual assault. Some older citizens considered the centre a no-go area on Fridays and Saturdays and, if they went out for meals at smart restaurants like Brasserie Blanc or the Chesil Rectory, made sure they were home early. Fed up with having their shop windows kicked in, the "BID" organization had arranged for comprehensive surveillance.

The pictures couldn't have been clearer. Ben had been pretty much the only person in town on that late Monday evening. Bird and Jackson could follow his every move. He walked through the train station car park, through the dingy underpass under the rail tracks, down the hill of Station Approach and along City Road past the Gurkha Chef. Then, he turned right into Jewry Street, had a quick look in the churchyard, then walked along to Barclays Bank at the end and left down the High Street. At the Butter Cross, he turned right through the alley that led to the cathedral, past the Slug and Lettuce and the Eclipse, both long closed for the night. Near the Statue Of Light, in the cathedral grounds, he paused to talk to someone, who was seen shaking his head. Ben then walked back to the High Street before turning right and ending up leaning on the parapet of the bridge by the City Mill, staring into the clear, fast flowing waters of the Itchen. After a moment, he seemed to make a decision, and quickened pace along Eastgate Street before stopping outside the very building where they were watching the footage, North Walls Police Station.

Jackson paused the tape.

"Okay, so how do you interpret this?"

"Well, he's not just going for a stroll, and he's not running away. He seems to be looking for someone or something. He keeps stopping and peering into dark places."

"Yes, and there's only one person he could be looking for."

"Corey Zander."

"And you know what that means."

"Yes. It means he doesn't know that Corey is dead. Which, in turn, means that he can't have killed him."

"Unless... Is it too far-fetched to suspect that he is trying to make us think that? He's lived here for years so he'd know about the CCTV system. And he's a bright lad."

Bird thought for a moment. "Look at this. He stops outside here and walks up and down for two minutes, deciding whether to come in. What does that mean?"

"Okay, let's look at the two possibilities. Scenario One: he's killed Corey and now has the presence of mind to walk around making it look as if he doesn't realize he's dead. In that case why would he even think of coming to the police station? Unless, of course, he wants to confess, in which case, why the wild goose chase?"

"And if we rule that option out, what is Scenario Two?"

"Scenario Two is this: He genuinely is searching for Corey Zander. When he gets here, he has to decide whether to report him missing or not. He knows that Zander has a track record of disappearing after concerts and turning up safe and sound in the morning. So Walker decides not to bother us, and goes home to bed."

"Which the CCTV confirms."

"Yes, and that means that Walker is definitely innocent."

"Great. We're back at square one."

"Not really. We have another obvious suspect, more obvious, really. We need to interview Barry Mort."

Chapter 7

English society can be difficult to comprehend. Even in the 21st-century, it is riddled by class divisions. So, nestling alongside the mansions of Chilbolton Avenue, with their huge, high-fenced gardens backing onto the golf course, could be found the community of Stanmore. Built in the 1930s as a council estate, it was an attractive area. Solid, red-brick semis straggled up the steep-sided hill and enjoyed panoramic views over St. Catherine's Hill and the M3 cutting. It looked like a really nice place to live.

About half of the inhabitants were in "social housing". Many of them were salt-of-the-earth, hard-working people with low incomes. Some had large families. Others on the Stanmore Estate had taken advantage of Margaret Thatcher's reforms, which encouraged people to buy their council houses. These were "owner-occupiers", who tended their gardens assiduously and maintained their houses with a view to resale value. Then, there were the many students who had arrived in droves in recent years, due to the rapid expansion of the university. They lived in "properties of multiple occupancy", which were ex-council houses, bought by people like Diana Leighton as an investment, and split up into three, four or even five separate dwellings. Students, bless them, didn't have a lot of time to spend keeping things neat and tidy.

So, Stanmore, once a cohesive community, was quite a mixture, the main thing the residents having in common being a lack of wealth. And so, it had a reputation. To outsiders, it was not the sort of place you'd walk on your own at night. It had its fair share of problems and troublemakers. Its street names featured more than other areas in the "In The Courts" column of the Weekly News. Drug dealing, major and minor; petty theft; disputes between neighbours; domestic incidents; all of these fitted into the image, justified or not, that Stanmore had in the area.

So it was with a sigh of resignation that Bird identified Barry Mort's address as Thurmond Road, Stanmore. It didn't take long to find the address, as there was plenty of documentation to hand about Mort's history. Bird leafed through a few cases. In 1999, while still a teenager, Barry had been convicted for arson. He'd taken against a fellow pupil at Kings' School and stuffed a firework through his parents' letterbox at their house on nearby Badger Farm. He'd received a suspended sentence and an admonishment to change his ways.

The next case Bird found was a brawl outside the Porthouse nightclub in Middle Brook Street. One of Mort's mates had spotted a guy from Portsmouth looking at his girlfriend and had laid into him, just the sort of incident the CCTV network had been set up to combat. By now, Mort had hooked up with a few other problem kids from the area and the concept of the "Mort Gang" had become known. Mort and his friends had been ejected by the bouncers but the hapless visitor, leaving the club at 1 am, had been jumped on by the waiting gang outside McDonald's. Video footage had clearly shown Mort stamping on the victim's head. For this, he had received his first custodial sentence.

Bird continued looking through the case documents. Mort was clearly involved with drugs. He had minor convictions for possession and a major one for distribution of class A drugs, crack to be precise. But the main way in which he was a menace to society was extreme violence after excessive consumption of alcohol. One case was of particular interest to Bird, as he had been peripherally involved in it as a junior investigating officer.

In July 2006, the city's annual Hat Fair was coming to a close. This was a festival of street theatre for which Winchester was renowned. For a long weekend, the streets were filled with musicians, clowns, illusionists, jugglers, comedians and acrobats, all of them performing for free but hoping that passers-by would put money in their hats (after which the festival was named). As it was a Saturday night, a few lads from Southampton had pitched up in town. A band was playing on a makeshift stage in front of the Guildhall and people were dancing.

The Southampton guys got a bit boisterous and one of them, while dancing, accidentally elbowed a Winchester bloke called Ray Matthews in the stomach. A few punches were thrown but it soon calmed down and the party continued; however, Matthews was still angry and wanted revenge. He walked down the High Street to a pub where Barry Mort and his mates were playing darts. Matthews told Mort what had happened, and within minutes, Mort and his mates were back in the Broadway. One of Mort's mates lived in the city centre, so, as they passed, they picked up weapons from his flat in the form of a hammer and a crowbar. Without hesitation, Mort walked straight up to the guy Matthews pointed out and smashed him on the head with the crowbar, knocking him unconscious.

Apart from the fact that it turned out he had hit the wrong person, in Barry Mort's warped mind, he had only meted out justice. However, there were numerous witnesses who had seen it all, and the judge saw it differently, sentencing him to three and a half years and pointing out that the victim was lucky not to have been brain-damaged or even killed. He sincerely hoped that Mort would have learned his lesson that violence was never acceptable.

It was this case that Bird and Jackson were mulling over as they slowly negotiated the speed bumps of Stanmore Lane on the drive to visit Barry Mort. As far as they could ascertain, he had remained unemployed since last being released from prison, so ought to be at home.

"I don't like to jump to conclusions," said Jackson, in what Bird took to be a direct reference to the over-hasty arrest of Ben Walker, "but it looks very much as if Mort is our man. The Hat Fair case is almost identical: hitting someone you don't like over the head with a blunt instrument when you're drunk. Premeditated, too."

"And I don't like to stereotype people," replied Bird, "but I've met Mort before, and he's going to fulfill every prejudice you may have."

A small woman in her 30s opened the door. Her hair was scraped back off her forehead into a ponytail and she wore pink jogging bottoms and a fake Hollister sweatshirt.

"Good morning. Is Barry Mort at home?"

"What do you want? If it's about the council tax, we paid it yesterday."

Bird produced his ID card.

"Hampshire Constabulary. We'd like a quick word, just some enquiries we're making."

"Baz," the girl called up the stairs. "Someone wants to speak to you. Guess what, it's the police."

Footsteps clumped down the stairs and Barry Mort appeared, pretty much as Bird had remembered him. He had a red, unshaven face and a shaved head with two earrings in each ear. His off-white singlet vest revealed both arms tattooed from wrist to shoulder and disappearing down his chest. A spider's web pattern covered his neck. When he opened his mouth, his teeth were uneven and brown and even at a metre's distance, his breath smelt of last night's tobacco and alcohol. The look he gave them was a mixture of defiance and scorn.

"Police? What have I done now? Why me? I ain't done nothing."

"That's okay, because we're not accusing you of anything. We'd just like to ask you some questions."

Barry sighed and opened the door for Bird and Jackson to enter a front room which was pretty much what they had expected; yes, those self-fulfilling stereotypes again. There were empty cans of White Lightning cider lying around among the cartons of not-quite-finished Domino's pizza. Clothes hung steaming on a clothes rack in front of a gas fire. The house was obviously populated by heavy smokers, because the smell was overwhelming. Thank goodness, there didn't appear to be any children in this relationship, because heaven help any little mite having to crawl around amongst all the junk. Peering into the kitchen and looking at the crockery piled up in brown water in the sink, Bird hoped they wouldn't be offered any tea; on the other hand, Barry and his partner didn't seem to be the tea-offering types.

"So what do you think we're here about?"

"That fucker who tried to strangle me at The Station. I'm glad you're here. I was going to come down to you and get you to charge him, but I knew you'd just try to blame me for it. With my record, I'd have ended up getting charged instead of him."

"Don't you think we may be here looking for drugs?"

"You can look all you like but you won't find any. Listen, I promised I was going to stay out of trouble and I will. Prison is shit. I won't have any drugs in the house because I've had therapy and I've changed. Shelley is pregnant" – oh God, there was indeed a little bump there, Bird noticed – "and I'm not going back in."

"I've got witnesses who say you were drunk, violent and aggressive on Monday night. Is that your idea of starting a new life?"

Barry looked, as far as he was able, abashed. He clearly knew he had some explaining to do.

"Why don't you tell us what you remember about Monday night?"

"It was shit. My anger management mentor told me that a few beers were okay but nothing more. The problem was that I won £200 on a bet at Stan James. I put money on a horse called "Mortified" and it came in at 100 to one."

"So that was good, not shit."

"It was then, but I went to a pub to celebrate. I called some friends to come down and before I knew it, I drank too much and was getting lairy."

Jackson remembered seeing a dispute at an Indian restaurant being logged in the incident book.

"It wasn't you lot at the Gandhi, was it?"

"Yeah, bastards tried to overcharge us, or that's what I thought. I'm not a racist, but…" His voice trailed off. "Anyway, I remembered my cousin Gary said he was playing at The Station so we all went up there."

"We've been told you tried to barge in without paying."

"I wasn't fucking going to pay to see my own cousin, you're joking. Cunt wanted fifteen quid, no fucking chance."

Like so many English people, Mort seemed completely unaware of any possible offence his almost uninterrupted use of swearwords might cause. He obviously moved in circles where this was completely normal, but Bird at least tried to tone him down a bit.

"Barry, please moderate your language before you continue."

Mort seemed startled by the request, but at least offered, "Sorry, mate."

"I'm not your mate," thought Bird, but didn't want to interrupt the flow.

"Okay, so you're in there, what happens?"

"I quite liked the band, they were good. Then we went out for a smoke."

"So why did you come back?"

"I don't know. We had a few more pints while that fat Yank was singing, Cornish Wafer or whatever his name is."

"Had you seen him before? I'm trying to work out why you went back in."

"Yeah, I met him outside earlier on. He was going out the front door when I wanted to come in. He was so fat, he nearly pushed me over. So I pushed him. I get funny when I've been drinking, that's why I'm cutting down. I was going to hit the fucker, but my mates stopped me. So later on, I thought I'd go in and see what he sounded like, he seemed a right cunt to me."

"So what happened?"

"He was singing that shit old song," Barry laughed. "What's it called?

Shag My Dad? It was crap, he wasn't even in tune. All I did was heckle him a bit, and then he went for me."

"He attacked you?" This was a novelty, someone attacking Barry for a change. Bird had already heard descriptions of the scene from others, but he wanted Barry's version.

"Fucker had me up against the wall. He's a big fucker, – er – bloke, and he's strong. I nearly passed out, then he suddenly let me go and walked out. I'd have gone after him but I couldn't breathe."

This pretty much tied in with everything that everyone else had said so far, but Barry was in full flow now.

"Anyway, why are you talking to me about this? All I did was shout out a few rude comments. That cunt tried to bloody strangle me. He's the one you should be arresting."

Jackson looked at Bird, then both of them looked back at Mort.

"Don't you know?"

"Know what?"

"Haven't you seen the news? Has no one told you?"

"What?"

"We can't question Corey Zander. Someone killed him in the car park of The Station."

Silence. Shelley moved in and took Barry's arm. "You don't think Barry done it? He ain't like that any more."

Mort's mouth was wide open. "No, no, no. I shouted a bit, that's all, and he attacked me."

Bird looked at him. His response certainly seemed genuine, but to him it looked like the regrets of a guilty person, who'd been found out.

"Here's how it looks to us. You were drunk, violent and aggressive. You have a record for assaulting people with weapons like iron bars. We think there's a good chance you killed Corey Zander and we'd like you to come with us."

....

Southampton Airport at Eastleigh was surprisingly busy at 6am, full of business travellers setting off to Amsterdam, Paris and the Channel Islands. Even at this time of day, there was plenty of traffic on the M3, so Ben had cut along the back road through Twyford and Allbrook.

The display monitors went from "On Time" to "Landed" to "Luggage In Hall". Ben had distinct butterflies. The situation was unprecedented and he had no idea how to deal with it. No words he could come up with could possibly be appropriate. He tried rehearsing a few phrases of sympathy, but nothing seemed to fit.

Passengers started to stream through, mainly men in suits, carrying laptops. There was no mistaking Lucy Cruz. A slight, slim figure in jeans, her ash-blonde hair, with a fringe, was sculpted into two pigtails. She pulled a little green suitcase on wheels, like a mini version of her father's luggage. Ben hadn't made a card this time, confident that she would stand out among the business people. He walked forward, holding out his hand, but he hadn't reckoned on Lucy being American. Her embrace was close, her body almost childlike as Ben found himself, very un-Britishly, putting his arms around her. Her body shook as she sobbed. For 48 hours, she'd needed to release her emotions on somebody, and the time had come.

Ben found himself leading the way to the car park, pulling the suitcase and with Lucy attached to his arm. It felt strange but, in among the jungle of mixed emotions, it felt good. On the way back to Winchester, he tried to explain what had happened in a way that would make some sort of sense.

"So they accused you of killing my dad? Are they crazy?"

"Well, they just went for the nearest suspect, but now I think they're feeling a bit foolish."

"So what about this Mort maniac? He sounds like a total douche bag."

"He is, and if they don't investigate him, I'm going to go in and kick up a hell of a fuss."

Corey's body was in the mortuary at the Royal Hampshire County Hospital in Romsey Road. As next of kin, Lucy's role would be to carry out the formal identification and the time had been set for three-thirty that afternoon. In the meantime, Ben was unsure what to do. First, he drove to North Walls, where he introduced Lucy to DCI Bird. This was his first meeting with Bird since being charged, so Bird took the opportunity to apologize for jumping the gun.

"Well, cheers," replied Ben. "You might as well apologize for pretty well ruining my life. The whole town thinks I'm a criminal. 'No smoke without fire', 'Mud sticks', you know what they're all saying."

Bird resorted to the standard line. "I'm sorry sir. I was only doing my job."

Lucy just looked at the floor. The grief, the craziness, the politics and the practicalities all combined into a perfect storm of baffling intensity, as Bird explained her duties. After the body had been formally identified and the pathologist's report had been filed, the body could be released for her to arrange for repatriation. Horrible, it sounded like the fate of a soldier in Afghanistan or something.

Ben didn't know what to do about accommodation for Lucy. There was no room at his place and his relationship with Robert was now such that he couldn't ask him and Diana. On the other hand, hotels in Winchester were prohibitively expensive and he knew Lucy wasn't well off. In the end, he found Bed and Breakfast for £35 in the First Inn Last Out, a pub in Easton Lane that had garnered a terrible reputation in a recent hotel makeover programme on TV. It wasn't ideal, but it would have to do, so he dropped a jet-lagged, tired and drained Lucy off there, promising to return at 3 pm.

Ben's next stop was school. He could put it off no longer. Robert was on playground duty but got another member of staff to take over when it was obvious that the children, whispering and pointing, were disturbed by Ben's presence. Even the other teachers avoided meeting Ben's eyes.

"I've come to ask if I can be reinstated," said Ben, "in view of the fact that I'm no longer a suspect and the police have apologized."

"It's not up to me, I'm afraid," replied Robert, his tone resolutely formal, as if he and Ben were hardly acquainted. "The formal decision has to be made by the governors."

"How soon can they decide? Could I come back immediately, pending what they decide?"

"No. I'll have to organize another extraordinary meeting. It'll take a couple of days. In the meantime, you'll have to remain on suspension. Sorry, Ben."

Ben explained the situation to Lucy when he picked her up. At least it meant he was free to help her out as she went about her tasks, the first of which was to identify her father's body. It was raining, of course, as they paid for the hospital car park. Ben felt desperate as he sat on the red plastic chair in the stark, brightly-lit waiting room. He'd seen enough episodes of "Silent Witness" to well imagine the scene behind the closed door. An official would pull back the white, starched sheet over Corey's head, to reveal the grizzled, bearded features. Lucy would nod, silently, maybe kiss him one time, then step back as the shroud was replaced. It was a kind of situation most people would hope never to have the misfortune to find themselves in, and Ben could only guess at the desolate feelings which would be overwhelming Lucy.

"That must have been quite an ordeal."

"I knew it was him, and I tried to mentally prepare myself, but it was still a horrible experience," Lucy confided.

"I'm glad I was able to be here with you," said Ben. "I know it seems strange, but for some reason I feel I have a sort of affinity with Corey, even though he irritated the hell out of me."

"He irritated everyone," laughed Lucy, "but I'm glad you're here too."

Their first stop was The Station. They had to collect Corey's possessions, such as they were: the guitar, the effects pedals, the CDs and the remaining clothes and bits and pieces in his suitcase, which included a battered copy of Willy Vlautin's novel "The Motel Life".

Then they drove on to Chilbolton Avenue, where Ben introduced Lucy to Diana. Diana did her best to be comforting, describing how Corey had sung to her on the patio only a few days before. "It wasn't really my sort of music, but it was very kind of him." Lucy was impressively willing to put a good face on, being polite and friendly to Diana and even managing the odd smile.

Ben and Rosie had agreed, by phone, that they couldn't subject Lucy to an evening alone in her tiny room at the B & B, so Ben took her back to their flat, where Rosie made spaghetti bolognese and the three of them tried to make sense of all that had happened. Small talk didn't seem appropriate, but Ben did suggest a few nice places in the area they could visit while waiting for Lucy's return flight with her father's remains.

The morning was spent at R. Steele and Partners, the undertakers in Chesil Street. It was obvious that the simplest and most practical arrangement would be for a cremation, and for Lucy to transport the ashes herself back to Texas in her bag. This was preferable to having a coffin transported by plane, and also cheaper and less prone to red tape. A slot was booked for Friday at 1pm at Basingstoke Crematorium, an unlikely location for the last journey of a man from Oklahoma, but the nearest facility there was. Corey had come a very long way from Tahlequah.

In the afternoon, Ben took Lucy to one of the places he'd mentioned. He figured that she might like to see the kind of countryside she wouldn't find in Texas, so he drove over to Bursledon, where the two of them walked for miles along the path that skirts the Hamble River. The sun decided to make a showing, as they walked along the shingle path past the skeleton-like wrecks of generations of wooden ships, revealed by the receding tide. They caught the little pink passenger ferry over to Hamble and stopped in a delicatessen for tea. Lucy wasn't exactly hungry, but made a half-hearted go at eating the toasted teacake that Ben bought her. "Typically English", he explained.

As they walked back, Lucy told Ben a little about her life in Austin with Corey.

"You couldn't say we were similar in many ways, but we were close, yes. In a way, I guess I was a kind of substitute wife or life partner."

"Am I right in thinking he didn't exactly have a healthy lifestyle?"

"He sure didn't! I was permanently worried about his eating habits, his lack of exercise, but what could I do? I didn't want to be over-protective towards him, although he looked out for me as a good dad should."

"Did he talk much about your mum?"

"Yes, he often said how much he regretted the way her life ended. He wondered if he could have done more to save her. That's why I'll never have anything to do with drugs."

Corey himself had fitted in well with the music community in Austin. There was plenty of work, both for him and for her. Once or twice, they'd staged their own attempts at "multimedia" shows, where her art works would be exhibited and Corey would play music to accompany them.

"We did one of those at the famous Waterloo record store in Austin, but it ended badly. It was real embarrassing. One of the staff complained that Dad had groped her. He was asked to leave, and it was just as well he did, because her redneck husband turned up just after he left. I had to stall him until Dad was well out of the way."

"Phew!"

"Dad was no angel," Lucy confirmed. "I think he'd have liked a longer-term relationship but nothing ever lasted. That wasn't the only time he got into trouble for interfering with women. One time, at my 21st birthday party, he tried it on with one of my friends and she threatened to call the cops."

Ben found it hard to imagine the overweight hobo he'd met having such an active libido, but thinking back to the cool Grams posters, maybe it sort of made sense after all.

After an early dinner in the Jolly Sailor, a waterfront pub that Ben rightly hoped Lucy would view as quaint (a "vegetarian option" was available), he dropped her back at the B&B. The arrangement was that she would need to get on with all the bureaucratic things that had to be done but that she could call Ben if she needed him. Unlike her dad, Lucy possessed a mobile phone.

The main events of the next few days were the Governors' Meeting and the funeral. For the crucial meeting, Ben dressed in his best suit and tie, but he knew it would be an uphill struggle. Just walking round Weeke, he'd established that news of his release without a stain on his character hadn't exactly convinced the local population. Mothers grabbed their children's hands and crossed the road to avoid him. Fathers gave him threatening looks. One teenager in a shell suit even spat pointedly on the ground as he walked past, narrowly missing Ben's shoe.

A brief conversation with Robert didn't help. Ben asked him for his support in asking to be reinstated.

"No can do, I'm afraid."

"But why not? I've done absolutely nothing wrong. It's not fair."

"Listen, Ben, I'm not daft. I found some stuff on the patio, brown stuff wrapped up in cellophane. I grew up in the sixties so I know what's what."

"But that's nothing to do with me."

"Isn't it? That's strange. Rosie told me you went all the way to Millbrook to get it for him."

Ben went briefly cold, then flushed in anger. He'd only told Rosie on the strict condition that she would never breathe a word about it.

"I take it your silence means you haven't got anything to say for yourself. The point is, you're tainted, Ben. It'll take me years to rescue the school's reputation as it is. No way can I recommend to the governors that you're a suitable person to remain employed at St John's."

And so it was. At the meeting, wracked with nerves to the extent that he could hardly speak, Ben explained that it had all been a mistake, that the police had acknowledged the error, that he was a dedicated teacher with a good track record and that there was no reason he shouldn't be reinstated. He brought his union representative with him, who agreed with all he said.

"If it was down to us, I'm sure there would be no problem," ruled the chairman of governors. "But we have the reputation and welfare of the school to consider. Feelings among parents and pupils are running high. Mud sticks, I'm afraid. And crucially, the head teacher feels unable to offer you support, so I'm sorry to say that your suspension is upheld."

And that was that. The NUT rep assured Ben that he would be able to appeal, that they didn't have a leg to stand on, and that lengthy litigation could ensue, but that he had a good chance of eventual victory. Ben, however, was completely demoralized and his reaction was to think along the lines of "stuff you, stuff your school, stuff your job."

Dinner back at the flat that evening was ultra-tense, as Rosie was now truly involved in the fallout. Ben was furious, not only at her betrayal, but at her father's behaviour. Both were inextricably linked and Ben now felt alone and abandoned.

"You promised not to tell him."

"I know, but he confronted me with the stuff and it just slipped out. He promised not to tell you I told him."

"Bloody hell, all this promising this and that and not telling this or that, it's like being back in the playground with the kids."

Truth to tell, Ben had been heartily sick of the job and the lifestyle anyway. During the course of the evening, he made the decision that the most dignified thing he could do was resign. He picked up his laptop and started to compose a letter to the governors.

....

The gathering at Basingstoke Crematorium was a small and bedraggled one. Inevitably, there was a persistent drizzle as mourners arrived and waited outside the chapel for the previous ceremony to finish. Robert and Diana had agreed to attend out of respect, and Ben, Rosie and Lucy travelled with them in Diana's Range Rover. Andy and Sam from The Station were there, as was Glenn Wallis. Glenn had told the local promoters about the tragedy and a couple of them had travelled up from Southampton and Portsmouth. Finally, the guy with the Grams' T-shirt was in attendance, without his wife.

Surreally, the ceremony was conducted by a rock 'n' roll vicar, a guy with a Brian May poodle cut who claimed to be aware of the Grams' work. He seemed quite star-struck to be given this "gig". The coffin entered to the sounds of the Grams' instrumental track "Desert Grave". The rocking vicar gave a well-researched speech, in which he summarized Corey's career and read out some tributes which he'd found on Facebook. "Rest in peace, brother," said Sam Baker. "Your songs will stay with me forever," said Caitlin Carey of Whiskeytown. Lucy, truly a fish out of water, somehow managed to read out a poem she'd written about what a great dad he'd been, and laid on the coffin a portrait of him she'd painted. And then, inevitably, the strains of "Mad And Bad" rang out as the curtains parted and Corey disappeared into the flames. You couldn't have made it up.

Chapter 8

The next few days, while the boxes were being ticked for Lucy to collect the ashes and take them back to Austin, gave her and Ben the chance to get more comfortable with each other. Ben had no job to go to so, as they waited, he took Lucy to other places in the area that he thought she might like. He started with Farley Mount, the beauty spot he'd hoped to show Corey.

"You see that strange pyramid-shaped monument? It's in memory of a horse called 'Beware Chalk Pits' which fell into a pit in 1733 while foxhunting. Am I boring you?"

Lucy's bright eyes showed he wasn't.

"Your dad didn't seem interested at all. I was looking forward to showing him round."

"Well, I'm making up for that. It's great!"

One day, they walked all along the Itchen Navigation towpath, starting near Winchester College, where Lucy was thrilled to see the house where Jane Austen had died. From there, they walked through the Water Meadows, past Shawford Lock. Ben explained that children liked to swim there in the summer, and for a moment, he thought that Lucy was about to strip off and plunge in, but she restrained herself.

As they strolled on in the watery sunshine, Ben drew the line at exposing Lucy to Eastleigh, home of Benny Hill and the Tornadoes' Heinz Burt, and instead, they followed the Navigation all the way to Southampton, struggling through waist-high nettles to a pub called the Fleming Arms, where a plaque confirmed that Bob Marley and the Wailers had played there in May, 1973. "Who'd have thought it?" enthused Lucy. "Ben, you're the perfect host."

Although Lucy was older than Ben and from a notably different background, they seemed to get on. After all, they had a lot to talk about, ranging from the practicalities of their situation, to the kind of quite deep conversation about life and death, provoked by the circumstances, that strangers don't normally have with each other. He hardly saw Rosie during this period, so had no idea what she might have thought about him spending time with Lucy. He'd not forgiven Rosie for the indiscretion which had cost him his job.

Lucy found a return route on the internet which was less complicated: a flight from Heathrow via Minneapolis. In a move which seemed to draw a line of symmetry with the trip only a couple of weeks earlier to collect Corey, Ben drove up the M3 and round the M25 once more. As they hugged farewell at the entrance to Security, agreeing that they would remain in touch, the two of them kissed for the first time. It just seemed okay and Ben, at least, felt that one chapter of the story was closing, as he watched Lucy disappear, the urn with Corey's ashes safely in her rucksack. Lord knew what Security were going to make of that, but Lucy had done her research and had the required customs certificate from the crematorium in her pocket. At least the heavy CDs were in Corey's old suitcase, safely in the hold.

....

Barry Mort's anger management course was proving its worth. Frustrated and inwardly furious, he managed to refrain from shouting and lashing out as the interrogation began. A duty solicitor by his side, he mainly looked down, sighing a lot, as he answered Bird's questions with apparent honesty.

"You will be aware, Barry, that we already have your DNA on file. Can you tell us why Corey Zander's coat has got your DNA all over it?"

"Yes, I can. I already told you that he attacked me. He had his bloody hands round my throat. I was struggling, trying to push him away. I thought he was going to strangle me. So of course I touched his jacket, loads of times."

Bird pulled out the Grams' button badge again and laid it on the table.

"There are several fingerprints on this badge, and one of them is yours. How did it get there?"

"Just the same way. I was pushing his chest, trying to get him to stop. I'm sure I touched that stupid badge, so of course my prints on it."

"So talk me through what happened, starting from when you entered the room."

"I already told you I was drunk, and I'm sorry about that. I've kept out of trouble because of Shelley. But I won that money and then..." He paused. "I don't know why, but that Yank just got on my tits. All I did was shout out a few things and he just went for me."

"Why do you think he let you go?"

"I don't know. He just suddenly dropped me and walked out."

"And what did you do?"

"I just sat there for a while, then I went after him."

"Ah, so you're admitting you went after him."

"No, no, I don't mean I 'went after him' in the way you meant. He just went, and then I went."

"Where were your mates while all this was going on?"

"Dean was in the garden having a fag and Jason was in the front bar talking to my cousin. They never came in at all."

"No, but I bet you asked them to help you get revenge on Corey."

"Listen, I keep telling you, I didn't want no trouble. That cunt grabbing my throat sobered me up, no problem. I just wanted to get away, and I couldn't see him anywhere anyway. I didn't want to see him. I was fucking bricking it, he's a big bugger."

"Maybe, but the three of you could have taken him out. Two to hold him and one to hit him."

"I said we should just go. We were pissed off, yes, but we wanted to get away."

"Someone told us you were shouting abuse at him as he ran away."

"Yeah, I expect I did, he was a cunt. But I was just... you know, shouting. That's what you do when you're angry."

"So answer this carefully, Barry. We have several witnesses who have told us that, as you left the room, you clearly said, and I quote, 'I'm going to effing kill him'."

Mort looked genuinely cowed and haunted when he heard this. Was it a sign of guilt? Both Bird and Jackson thought it could be. As far as they were concerned, Mort had definitely killed Corey Zander in a drunken rage, with or without the help of his friends. He fitted the profile exactly. He had a record, he had motivation and he had opportunity. He certainly had no alibi, as he admitted being at the scene.

Mort spoke quietly. "Yeah, I know I said it, but I didn't mean it like that. It's just something you say. If I had murdered everyone I said that to, half of fucking Winchester would be dead." He hesitated. "Anyway, how was he killed? Stabbed? Shot? I ain't got a knife and I ain't got a gun."

Blimey, thought Bird, this guy is cleverer than he seems. He's trying to convince us he doesn't know what the murder weapon was.

"I think you know exactly how he died, Barry."

Despite his clear guilt, there were a couple of things that might potentially stand in the way of conviction. They'd identified Ben Walker's fingerprints on the bin, but the rest was just a blur of hundreds of unidentifiable prints from people opening the lid. Although the investigating officers were sure that Mort or one of his friends had dropped the brick in there and dragged the body behind it, there was no concrete evidence. The brick, too, had no tales to tell. It had been touched probably by every band that had ever propped that stage door open, but of Mort's DNA there was no trace. Nevertheless, Mort had to be their man, so he was remanded in custody. Bail was not granted. This man had a proven record of violence.

....

Bound up in the practicalities of sorting out the debacle which had overwhelmed him, Ben hadn't had much time to consider his future. Now, as he sat alone in the flat, things felt dark and frightening. He was being ostracized by his colleagues and neighbours. Robert had withdrawn his support, and Diana, even if she had wanted to, would never have gone against Robert's wishes. Rosie had betrayed him, and now new, unexpected elements were creeping in. Threatening messages were starting to appear on his Facebook page: "Tell the filth too much and you're dead"; "You did it, not Baz"; "Stay away from our kids, you paedo". Ben bitterly regretted clicking "Accept" to people he may have met in pubs over the years, but in reality hardly knew. Worse, a Facebook page called "Barry Mort is innocent" had been set up by his girlfriend Shelley. Like a fool, Ben took a look at it and instantly regretted it. It was full of references to Ben as "scum", "killer", and "grass". One message simply said, "Be afraid, Ben Walker. We're coming for you." It had 63 "Likes".

When Rosie came in from work, it was time to talk. She had had plenty of time to think things over and her mood was contrite.

"I can't tell you how ashamed and embarrassed I am at the way my father is behaving. And I've made things worse. I feel as if I've betrayed you. Believe me, Ben, of course I love my parents, but our relationship is more important than anything and I'll always stand by you."

She was so sincere that Ben was moved to forgive her and start again.

"There's nothing to be gained from going over the past. I have to admit that I feared our relationship was doomed, but surely we'll be stronger if we stick together."

"Of course we will."

They both cried and held each other. They were aware that, whatever happened, a courtroom ordeal lay ahead for Ben and that he'd need support.

"Our wedding will go ahead anyway, even if Robert refuses to come."

"He won't refuse to come. I'm his daughter and he loves me."

At the end of the emotional conversation, they'd even agreed a date: Saturday, May 25, and a place: Littleton Church, if it was available. Ben hadn't anticipated a church wedding, but Rosie had her heart set on it and Diana would have been inconsolable at the thought of a mere registry office event, even if her friends deigned to attend the wedding of a "criminal". As they went to sleep, some light seemed to be appearing at the end of the proverbial tunnel.

In the morning, that light disappeared. Three smashed eggs adorned the kitchen window and a spray painted message had appeared on the front door: "Ben Walker = Shit". Even in custody, Barry Mort's tentacles were reaching out. One thing was clear: wherever Ben's future lay, it wasn't in Winchester.

Ben suddenly realized that, with all that had gone on, he had completely omitted to contact his parents. Mid-morning, he phoned his mother in Chew Magna. What he had to tell her was so far outside her scope of experience that she was almost lost for words, but instinct kicked in: "That's all right, dear, you can come here for a while." An exchange of texts with Rosie confirmed the plan. He would go to the West Country, while she would relocate for the time being to Chilbolton Avenue. She couldn't stay in Taplings Road; it was only a matter of time before some lunatic would push something flammable through the letterbox.

....

In Austin, Lucy took a while to adjust to the emptiness of the house she had shared with her father so many years. Her exhibition at the Yard Dog Gallery had gone ahead as planned and some of her work had actually been sold, which gave her a financial cushion for a while. As she had feared, there was no sign of a will and, as far as she could work out, Corey hadn't even had a bank account. His entire lifestyle had been strictly "cash only". One of her first tasks was to contact Lance Wilson's sons, still running the "Lance-A-Lot" chain in East Oklahoma. They only had vague memories of Corey, but expressed their condolences, of course. The entire Wilson inheritance had gone to them, since Corey hadn't been Lance's son. She momentarily thought of asking for financial help, but pride ruled that out.

The community in Austin couldn't have been more supportive. The Austin American Statesman had already run an illustrated obituary, identifying him as one of the city's most respected musicians (surprising, as they had never run a feature on him before). Friends of Corey visited one after the other to pay their respects. Realizing that Lucy was likely to experience financial difficulties, all sorts of suggestions came out in conversation: a tribute concert; a CD of Corey's songs recorded by various friends; a "Kickstarter" campaign for Lucy herself to record some of his songs. This put a seed into Lucy's mind: might there be royalties still owing to Corey? She discussed this with Corey's friend Jon Dee Graham, who was quickly able to tell her the unwelcome truth: if he'd received no royalties in his lifetime, he certainly wouldn't get any after his death. The labyrinthine state of the music business meant that it would be impossible to trace where the money had been going. Expensive legal action might conceivably have brought results, but was it likely? Larry Goldberg, for example, had been dead for a decade. But what about the Chocs' and the Grams' back catalogues, freely for sale in all the local record stores, along with re-masters, reissues, compilations of demo tracks and live bootlegs? That, Jon assured her, was the nature of the music industry. Forget it.

One thing Lucy was able to do was replenish shops like Waterloo and End Of An Ear with stock of the "Corey Zander Live At The Saxon Pub" CD, which he'd hoped to sell on the UK tour. She'd half killed herself lugging them back from Winchester, but now she was glad she had; mysteriously, all stock of these rare items had suddenly sold out all over Texas. She made sure the transactions were done on a strictly documented Sale Or Return basis.

As for memorials, tributes and the like, Lucy put them on hold until she had time to consider all the possibilities. She couldn't even decide what to do with the ashes, so for the time being simply put them on the windowsill. For now, she needed to work. Strangely stimulated by the extreme events, she started to paint, draw and even – using her father's battered old acoustic guitar – write a few new songs.

....

Returning home, tail between legs, is a sobering experience for anyone. In his mid-twenties, settled in a good, if unexciting, career, Ben would not have expected to find himself being woken each day by his mother with a cup of tea, before being presented with a full English breakfast. His father was long retired and beginning to be rather frail. The couple were in a settled routine revolving around gardening, walking the dog, attending parish council and WI meetings and very occasional visits to the pub for meals. They listened to Ben's story with a complete lack of comprehension, but instinctively wanted to help him in his time of need.

"You can stay here as long as you want, dear," Mrs Walker assured him. Ben wasn't sure about that. Compared to Chew Magna, Winchester had been like Las Vegas, but what alternative did he have? He'd taken the car with him, so was able to travel to Bristol and Bath in search of work. In the short-term, he was still on full pay, but that would soon end. Besides, he needed to be occupied. Whenever he had nothing to do, confused and frightening thoughts would crowd in on him. Why had life decided to treat him so unfairly?

Ben now knew only too well what panic attacks were. One time, he came over faint in the Broadmead shopping centre in Bristol. He was confused by the artificial lights, the hubbub of noise and the crowds of people around him, and had to sit down on a bench or a few minutes to get his breath back. He almost felt as if he was having a heart attack, although he knew that was ridiculous.

On another, even more frightening, occasion, he'd had an attack of vertigo while walking across the Clifton Suspension Bridge. It was sunny afternoon in this lovely beauty spot and he wasn't feeling suicidal at all, but all of a sudden, he felt an almost irresistible urge to hurl himself off. Of course, generations of suicides in that spot had led to wire meshing being installed, making it quite impossible for anyone to jump, but it was frightening nonetheless. He had to crouch on the pavement for a while before he dared to continue, and several people cast him strange glances. What was that weirdo doing? Ben felt he wasn't in control of his own destiny, and when his mother found him weeping in the kitchen one night, she insisted on taking him to the family GP the next day.

Dr Kay was very understanding when confronted by an abridged version of why Ben had suddenly appeared in his surgery again for the first time since he was a child.

"It's only to be expected that you would feel unhappy and confused after what has happened to you. It's natural, Ben. I'm going to put you on antidepressants for a while, just a short-term thing until you get your life back on track."

The pills, some kind of Prozac affair, started to kick in within ten days and Ben set out to find some work. In Bradford-On-Avon, renovation work was being carried out on two of the locks on the Kennet and Avon Canal, which passed through the picturesque town. It was voluntary work, but it offered social interaction with a group of friendly, open-minded "alternative" types who liked to socialize in the evenings. Before he knew it, Ben found himself working behind the bar of a canalside pub called The Narrowboat, and not getting home until late at night. The doctor had said the trick to banish dark thoughts was to keep himself fully occupied and, together with the medication, it seemed to be working. He found his new set of friends a lot more stimulating than his ex-colleagues had been. He even found himself fancying a couple of girls on the project.

Ben's email exchanges and calls to Rosie were becoming just a little tedious. He wasn't really interested in Diana's latest amateur dramatic production and he certainly didn't care about Rosie's office gossip. As far as she could tell, things had calmed down in Winchester. With Ben no longer around, and no one having worked out the connection between him and Rosie, she wasn't being hassled. The media had lost interest for the time being, having reported Ben's release and the arrest of Barry Mort, and unsurprisingly failed to retract any of their previous inferences that Ben was the obvious suspect. In the meantime, police were clearly gathering and collating their evidence against Barry Mort, pending a trial sometime in the New Year. With a pang of something resembling resentment, Ben heard from Rosie that a full-time replacement for him had been appointed at St John's primary school. Robert, apparently, now harboured "no hard feelings". I bet he doesn't, thought Ben. He's not the injured party in all this.

More interesting were the emails from Lucy Cruz. Over the winter months, something like an old-fashioned penfriend relationship grew up. She appeared actually interested in the canal restoration work he would detail. She reported on the ideas and plans being mooted to commemorate Corey's life and updated him on the music scene in Austin in general.

"Everyone here is keen to do whatever they can to preserve Dad's memory. We're making all sorts of plans but nothing's fixed yet. How's the weather in Winchester? Non-stop sunshine here in Texas!"

It all sounded very exotic and very attractive, a true community based on communication and creativity. Ben was able to tell Lucy about a development in The Narrowboat.

"I've persuaded the landlord to let me run a weekly music night. I've booked a few West Country musicians like Jon Amor and Peter Bruntnell to do acoustic shows in the bar, and they're going down a storm. Let's hope no one gets murdered this time!" he found himself typing, his finger hesitating before hitting "Send". Would her sense of humour cope with this? Yeah, of course it would. And it did.

Rosie came over to visit a couple of times. She hoped to be introduced to his new friends, but Ben found excuses to avoid a meeting. Rosie, for some reason, insisted on wearing her smart estate agent's clothes even when not working. Would she fit in with his friends, more used to sporting dreadlocks and combat trousers and discussing their itinerant lives on canal narrowboats? Ben doubted it somehow. She did come to one of his music nights however, and enjoyed Neil Halstead's performance, even buying a CD for the car.

"He's got a really nice voice, he should go on X-Factor," she enthused.

"Hmm," thought Ben, "she really doesn't get it."

Rosie was keen to spend time discussing the exact arrangements for the wedding. Could her younger sister Natalie, away at university, be maid of honour? Fine. Could they afford to have the reception at Lainston House? No way. Had he given any thought to who to ask to be best man? This was awful, as Ben had absolutely no idea who to ask. Even with the Prozac, he felt terribly insecure. He felt that his participation in the wedding plans was half-hearted at best. Was he having doubts? He wouldn't have said so to Rosie, but yes. He knew that the life he had found was unsustainable in the long term, but for the first time in years, he felt comfortable, he felt that he "fitted in".

Ben spent Christmas Day working in The Narrowboat. He'd been offered double pay and it was hard to refuse. In fact, it was quite fun, serving turkey with all the trimmings to the old dears in their paper hats. On Boxing Day, he drove over to Winchester to spend the day with his future in-laws. Robert was in peace-making mode, bent on using the season of goodwill to smooth over their issues. Ben felt he had more to forgive than Robert did, but after a couple of post-lunch Drambuies, they shook hands and agreed, with varying degrees of sincerity, to let bygones be bygones. In Ben's mind, it was a total victory for the Leighton family, but Diana was delighted to "welcome Ben back to the family", and wedding plan-making went into overdrive for the rest of the day. Natalie joined in with alacrity and the only person not to be consulted at all was, inevitably, Ben.

In early January, Ben received an interesting and enticing email from Lucy in Austin. Had Ben ever heard of South By South West? Indeed he had. It was a massive music festival held in Austin each March. Ben had twice been to Glastonbury, but SXSW (as everyone knew it) was a completely different concept. It was held over a period of five days in hundreds of venues, large and small, all over the Texan capital city. It was also a music industry junket.

Lucy's question was this: In view of the fact that he'd shown Corey kindness and had been one of the last people to see him alive, would Ben like to attend the festival? The reason, she said, was that a tribute concert to Corey had been programmed as one of the key events at the festival. Far from the sadness associated with their last meeting, this was planned as a celebration of his life and music. "Go on, Ben," she concluded, "you know you want to."

It was irresistible. Ben booked the week of the 11th to 17th March off work and started trawling the internet for cheap flights. If he saved hard between now and then, he should be able to afford it. The only possible hindrance would be if the trial were to be set for that week, but Ben banished the thought. At last, he had something to look forward to.

Chapter 9

The police in Hampshire, meanwhile, were concentrating on putting together a watertight case to ensure the conviction of Barry Mort. There were plenty of other crimes that needed attention, but with a high-profile murder, it was essential to leave no holes in the evidence that could be exploited by a clever defence lawyer. Convictions too often collapsed because of some unanticipated technical loophole.

The first thing to look at in detail, when the team convened at the County Police Headquarters in Romsey Road, was the forensic evidence from the site. From the venue itself, there was the badly torn poster advertising a forthcoming appearance by the UK Subs. Fibres from Barry Mort's jacket were all over it, confirming what all witnesses had said, namely that he'd been forcibly held up against the wall by Corey Zander.

The essential items from the car park were the murder weapon, in the form of the brick, and the handle of the bin. The blood on the brick was definitely Corey's, but there was no proof that Mort had held the brick. It was so scarred from use that fingerprints were just a jumbled mess, and of Barry's DNA there was no trace. DNA swabs were also taken from his sidekicks, Dean Harris and Jason Bright, but these drew a blank as well. The obvious explanation was that Mort had worn gloves, and in the end it was decided that this would be the argument to present in court. A full search of Mort's house in Thurmond Road had produced no sign of any gloves, but he could easily have burnt them somewhere or dumped them in a bin on his way home. The budget didn't run to searching every possible bin and hedge on all of the several routes he could have taken home from The Station.

The question of who had dumped the brick in the bin was equally difficult to answer with certainty. The jumbled hotch-potch of smeared prints meant it was impossible to establish whether any of the gang had touched it. There was no DNA from any of the three. But wearing gloves was the likely explanation for that. All in all, there was no proof that any of them had opened the lid and dumped the weapon; but on the other hand, there was no proof that they hadn't.

Corey's clothes substantiated the team's suspicions. His scruffy coat contained everything they suspected, Mort's DNA, fibres from his jacket, and, of course, the fingerprint on the badge. Corey's shirt collar was drenched in his own blood.

Barbara Sellars then talked everyone through the pathologist's report on Corey Zander. Dr Patel had opened the body up and confirmed minor signs of liver disease and the previously documented heart repair evidence, but the cause of death clearly lay elsewhere.

"She says that he suffered a major brain haemorrhage, caused by the back of his head connecting with a hard object. The shape of the imprint area is consistent with it having been a house brick; dust particles confirm that. The blow could have been inflicted by someone hitting him with the brick, but it could also have come from the victim falling, or being pushed backwards and falling onto it."

"Could it have just been a simple accident?"

"She says it's unlikely, because a natural cause of falling over, such as tripping or feeling faint, would have meant a forwards falling motion, in which case the wound would most likely have been on the front of the head." When all the pathologist's evidence was presented to the coroner, he had no choice but to bring in a verdict of manslaughter or murder by persons unknown; it had quite clearly not been an accident.

Now it was time for formal interviews with all the other witnesses. The immediate top priority was to attempt to eliminate the other two members of Mort's gang on the night. Both were dodgy characters with minor criminal records of their own. They could easily have been involved in helping their friend avenge his humiliation, in which case they would at the very least be accessories and, at worst, be on murder charges themselves.

First to come in was Dean Harris. A skinny, pale faced, ferret-like man, his background was in drug dealing, and it showed. It was evident that he had a habit himself and he admitted as much, sweating and twitching as the interview went on. Harris had been smoking in the garden when Mort ran out of the venue.

"What was the first you knew about the trouble?"

"We was talking to Baz's cousin in the garden and Baz went back in. Then he comes running out and says we've got to go. I says 'Why?' and he says that Yank was coming to get him. So we all ran into the train station car park and then down Stockbridge Road."

"Did you see the American?"

"Yeah, he came out first. He went into the car park and just disappeared. That's why we took the chance and ran for it."

Next in was Jason Bright. Bright by name, but not by nature, thought Jackson, as he looked at the spotty face with the unfocused eyes and drooping lower lip. If anything, he had even less to tell. He'd been in the front bar, talking to Mort's cousin and playing the quiz machine, he said, before joining the others in the garden. This seemed implausible in view of the IQ level he seemed to possess, but his fingerprints were, indeed, on the machine in question. There had been a couple of other men in the bar, playing pool, but they had left shortly after Bright had, and had never been traced.

When questioned in detail, Bright's story exactly tallied with that of Harris. Barry Mort had suddenly burst out of the back bar and shouted to him and Harris to come with him, quick. Then they'd all three run off together.

"Where did you go?"

"We all ran into the train station car park and then down Stockbridge Road."

The interview transcript confirmed the use of identical words by Bright and Harris. They'd obviously planned in detail, probably with Mort, for their stories to corroborate each other, but did this mean they were lying? Bird was almost sure they must have been involved in some way, but there was absolutely no evidence to support his suspicions. Neither of the men had any fibres, DNA or fingerprints to suggest they had had any contact with Corey Zander at all. There was nothing to connect them to the brick or the bin either. If they were accomplices to the murder, there was no proof and no prospect of getting any. To accuse either of them of being involved risked muddying the waters and increasing the chances of an acquittal for Mort. On that basis, neither Harris or Bright were arrested and both were allowed to go.

Looking at the possible timeline, the investigating team concluded that the following had happened. Corey Zander had stormed into the car park and was standing there in the dark, fuming. Mort, having regained his breath but still drunk, angry and eager for revenge, had announced that he was going to kill Zander and also claimed to have "gone after him". It could easily be – and this was the most likely scenario – that he'd found Zander standing there looking the other way and had simply smashed him on the head with the first weapon he could grab. This was the sort of cowardly act of violence that Mort was known for. The other, less likely, possibility was that there'd been some kind of fight between them and that either Mort had pushed him, or that he had slipped and fallen over backwards onto the brick, as the pathologist had acknowledged was feasible.

The first possibility would mean a murder charge for Mort, but in the second case, manslaughter would be the more likely charge if a conviction was to be secured, because Mort would argue that it had never been his intention to kill Corey. In an effort to see if any clarification was available, the team needed to re-interview everyone.

First, Ben Walker was invited up from Wiltshire to be questioned again. This time, the atmosphere was completely different, because he was no longer a suspect. Instead of being questioned about hypothetical actions that had never taken place, he was now able simply to describe what had happened. The trouble, from the police's point of view, was that Ben had only witnessed the preamble, in the form of the scuffle in the room. Ben confirmed the sequence of events. By the time of the incident there was hardly anyone left in the room, because the Bookworms' friends had all left. He'd made a half-hearted attempt to stop Barry Mort coming in the first time, but the second time, he'd pretty much abandoned the door because he'd been watching Corey, who was coming to the end of his set. Mort just marched in and immediately started causing trouble.

The useful things that Ben confirmed were that Mort had indeed been offensively abusive for no other reason than that he was a drunken lout. He had quite definitely shouted that he'd kill Corey and he'd run out in apparent pursuit of him.

"Why didn't you follow?"

"I don't know, a mixture of things. I obviously didn't really think he was going to kill him, and Corey was twice his size so he didn't need any help from me. But mainly, I was frightened. I'd never been involved in anything like that before and I was scared I might end up getting hurt myself."

"So you saw nothing of the events outside?"

"No, I stayed in the room and helped clear up. I expected Corey to come back, so when he didn't, I went to look for him. By the time I got outside there was no one there at all, apart from Andy the landlord, clearing glasses from the tables in the garden."

"Do you think the landlord could have had anything to do with the killing?"

"Why on earth would he? He's a good, honest guy, just trying to make a living. But ..."

Suddenly, a thought sprang into Ben's mind.

"There's something I haven't mentioned before."

Oh God, don't confess now, thought Bird. That really would mess everything up.

"Yes?"

"Well, I can't be sure, but I believe I saw Carl, the guy from Southampton who supplied some dope to Corey. Maybe there's some connection there?"

"Where did you see him?"

"I thought I spotted him in the gig, but it could have been someone else."

"Was he in the garden?"

"I don't think so. I only saw him for a second, and it might not have been him anyway."

Bird made a note to follow this up.

Robert Leighton didn't like being called back in for a second interview.

"Well, officer, as you already know, I can't tell you anything useful, so are you really sure you will need to call me as a witness? It would reflect very badly on the school."

"We may not need to call you, Mr Leighton, but some of the evidence will be circumstantial. For example, we need you to confirm whether or not Mort threatened to kill Zander."

Robert looked dismayed. He couldn't lie, but this would almost certainly put him down as a witness. "Yes, I'm afraid he did."

His explanation for not following Mort was the same as Ben's. He was scared and he didn't want to get involved. But the moment he thought things might have quietened down, he headed straight for the exit. The last thing his reputation needed was for him to have been seen to be involved, even peripherally, in a pub brawl. He'd got out as fast as he could.

"And when you went out, did you see anything?"

"Well…" Robert looked down and hesitated. "I may have seen something."

"What do you mean, you may have seen something? Either you did or you didn't."

"What I mean is that I saw something, but I don't know exactly what it was."

Bird sighed. "What, you mean it was a UFO?" He was getting irritated by this pompous man. "Go on, Mr Leighton, spit it out, please."

"What I saw was two people arguing in the car park. I could hear them, as well, but I couldn't hear what they were saying."

"And who were these two people?"

"That's just it. It was dark and I wouldn't be able to describe them. One was big and the other was smaller."

"Did one have an American accent, like Zander?"

"I couldn't make that out."

Bird was elated. At last, he not only had a witness with something to describe, it was also a credible witness, someone with standing in the community. But one thing bothered him.

"Why didn't you mention this when we interviewed you before?"

"Well, it's a bit embarrassing, but I really didn't want to get involved. If I could avoid having to give evidence in court, I'd prefer that. You know how people talk and I have to think about the reputation of the school. It's bad enough having a teacher involved, far less the headmaster."

"Well, I'm sorry, but you're involved now. Now we can pretty well guarantee you will be called as a witness, and an important one at that. So you'd better get used to it." Bird wasn't impressed by someone who clearly thought his public standing was more important than his integrity.

It was a different matter with Rosie Leighton. It only took minutes to confirm that she hadn't seen anything at all. Her headache had meant that she had gone home before the real trouble had kicked off. She blamed the headache on nerves caused by Barry Mort's initial invasion of the room, which she had found very upsetting and intimidating. She confirmed that his behaviour had been drunken and objectionable, but there were numerous other witnesses who could testify to that effect. Jackson briefly toyed with the notion of Rosie not going straight home, but instead lurking in the car park to attack Zander. The whole idea was laughable, so Jackson told Rosie that it was unlikely that she would be called as a witness.

The students who had come to see the Bookworms all told an identical story. They had completely missed the incident in the hall because they had been outside, chatting, smoking and discussing their performance. They hadn't wanted to see Corey Zander because they assumed the music would be old-fashioned. Had they seen Corey come out of the pub? No, but they had all witnessed Barry Mort rushing out, gathering his mates and running away, shouting abuse. Their accounts were all so uncannily similar that Bird was sure the Mort gang must have got to them too. None of them were any use to his case, but he feared that some of them were likely to be called as defence witnesses.

Of the people who had actually seen Corey attacking Mort, no one had anything to add. The man in the Grams' T-shirt was particularly vociferous. Not only had his ill wife nearly been knocked off her chair when Zander stood up, but, in his opinion, "one of the greatest musicians who ever walked this earth" had been callously murdered in a country which should have been showing him hospitality. "That thug did it, as sure as I'm sitting here," he declared. "He said he was going to kill him, and he did."

Jackson was dispatched to the tower block in Millbrook to locate and interview Carl, the drug dealer. It was an unproductive visit. Not only did Carl deny ever having dealt in drugs or heard of anyone called Corey Zander, but his mother was more than happy to swear that he had been at home with her all evening, watching television, on the day of the killing. As there was nothing to connect him to the case beyond a hunch by Ben Walker, Carl was put on the back burner.

Bird and his team now began to collate all the evidence and interviews they had accumulated, in preparation for a trial which they hoped would be scheduled for the spring. It was quite clear who had killed Zander, but, with no eye witnesses, the exact details remained a mystery. Now it would be in the lap of the gods whether Mort was convicted or not, probably down to procedural quirks. The charge was murder, with the possibility that the judge might recommend the lesser charge of manslaughter.

In Winchester, the community grapevine was functioning well. The "Barry Mort Is Innocent" Facebook page had over 200 followers. Many of the posts focused on the point that it was typical of Winchester that the middle class teacher who could equally well be guilty had been released without charge, while the working class lad was now being framed on account of his past.

One girl from Stanmore recognized Rosie in the High Street one afternoon and asked her where Ben was. Rosie explained that he had "gone away for a while".

"He'd better not come back, then," said the girl, "or you know what'll happen to him."

Ben was glad to be away. His new life in Bradford-on-Avon was agreeable to him, although he found it ironic that he had, by chance, become involved in music promoting again. Luckily, there were no such dramatic events in the sleepy market town, and all the music evenings passed without incident. His parents didn't mind having him around. His life would have to be on hold until the trial, about which he'd just received a letter, telling him it had been scheduled for April. After that would come the wedding, of course.

The agreement that Rosie and Ben came to was a charter to "move on".

After the trial, it would make no sense for Ben to remain in Winchester. He had no reason to. Whichever way it went, he would potentially be under threat. His relationship with Robert could never really return to how it had been before, although Robert's attitude had mellowed to the extent that he had declared himself willing to write him a reference that would be good enough to get him another teaching job. Ben wasn't sure he wanted to teach again, but that was a decision for the future. As it was, he and Rosie agreed that either she would move to Wiltshire to join him after the wedding, or that the two of them would up sticks and move to another part of the country altogether. Rosie herself was well-qualified and had an unblemished record, so should be able to find work anywhere.

Ben's thoughts were increasingly concentrated on his forthcoming trip to Austin. He found a flight direct from Heathrow to Houston, where he planned to hire a car and drive down Highway 35 to Austin, arriving on the Tuesday before the Thursday the festival opened. Looking at Google Maps, he could hardly contain his excitement. A couple of the musicians he had booked at The Narrowboat had played at South By South West in previous years and told him enticing stories about the warm climate, the cool people and the unending music. Life afterwards was going to be tough, he knew, but for now, he was sincerely hoping for a lot of fun.

Chapter 10

If he'd given a bit more thought to it, Ben mightn't have been so optimistic. He was, after all, going to be hanging out with someone who had been recently bereaved in the most horrible way. But he'd sensed a toughness and inner strength in Lucy Cruz that made him feel it would be all right. He couldn't explain it, but for some reason, he felt they had a kind of affinity. As he drove his surprisingly large hire car towards Austin, he couldn't wait to see her again.

Lucy had offered to let him stay in her house. From what he could understand, this would have meant sleeping in Corey's bed, which he thought was a bit ghoulish. Besides, he was only weeks away from getting married, so wasn't sure it would be appropriate to share a home with Lucy. Daft, really, and very British, because in the free and easy environment of Austin, nobody would have even noticed, far less cared. So Ben had booked himself into the Super 8 hotel on Highway 35, which his GPS system efficiently led him to.

As he stepped out of the air-conditioned car, the heat hit him like a steamroller. He'd once been on holiday to Greece, but this heat was something else, it was deeply penetrating and soul-warming, the perfect antidote to a chilly and damp English spring. He checked into his room, an enormous affair which contained, to his amazement, two huge Queen sized beds, as well as a massive TV, a writing desk, a large bathroom and the obligatory trouser press, plus a devastatingly effective air conditioning system. You didn't get hotels like that in Wiltshire.

Ben woke on Wednesday morning to a less than satisfactory breakfast of dishwater tea and a hard bagel with some gunge representing butter. As arranged, Lucy met him in the foyer, smiling as she ran towards him. The embrace lasted a little longer than expected, her arms around his neck as she kissed his cheek. He could feel her fragile body through the gossamer thin cotton dress she wore. Was he feeling a thrill of excitement, he asked himself? Don't be silly, you're almost a married man. But he was relieved, because he had half expected Lucy to appear with a musclebound hunky Texan boyfriend in tow.

Lucy laughed as Ben related his breakfast experience. "Don't worry, we'll sort that out tomorrow. But now we've got to collect your badge."

As she manoeuvred her pickup through the traffic towards the Austin Convention Center, Lucy explained what was going to happen. She'd listed Ben as "official staff", because he would be helping out with the tribute concert.

"Official staff? That sounds a bit scary."

"No problem, Ben. You won't have much to do."

The Convention Center was a huge, futuristic building in the middle of town. It was already crawling with people signing in and collecting their credentials. It was here, explained Lucy, that the "trade" part of the festival took place, with business seminars and keynote speeches by industry insiders. As if on cue, Ben nearly fainted as a tall figure in skinny black jeans strode past. It was Chrissie Hynde of the Pretenders, exuding that elusive star aura as she headed for some kind of meeting.

"Wow, she nearly touched me," enthused Ben.

"Almost, but not quite," deadpanned Lucy.

After a lengthy queuing session, Ben found himself in possession of a Platinum Pass, on a lanyard around his neck, complete with a mugshot of himself. "Ben Walker, staff", it declared. He'd rarely felt so important or, indeed, valued.

"You won't need that till tomorrow," said Lucy. "Today we're going to have some fun. I'm going to return your compliment and show you round. But in the next few days, you'll get to know every corner of Austin, so today we're going to explore the great outdoors."

Lunchtime found them basking in the sunshine on one of the balconies at the Oasis at Lake Travis, an outdoor restaurant consisting of tiers of decking clinging to the hillside above the glittering waters. Still jet-lagged and generally baffled at being in America for the very first time, just 48 hours after serving his last customer in The Narrowboat on a dingy, drizzly March evening in Wiltshire, Ben felt vaguely dizzy and strangely euphoric. A beer helped encourage that feeling. Lucy laughed as he ordered a Budweiser: "We don't drink that stuff here." The gourmet treat that was the chilli burger he tucked into was almost orgasmic. He'd truly never tasted anything like it, as it melted in his mouth in a guilty, cholesterol-packed ten minutes of culinary joy. Below them, speedboats criss-crossed the lake from jetties attached to mansions with swimming pools. Austin, explained Lucy, was Nirvana to dot com millionaires seeking the quiet life.

As they ate, Lucy told him more about the tribute gig. Ben's fears of a maudlin atmosphere melted away as Lucy explained the plans.

"We want it to be a positive, forward-looking event, packed with friends and fans. Initially, we were going to stage it at Antones. It's a big cavernous blues venue in Austin, really famous. But we got cold feet that we might not be able to fill it, so we've gone for the Saturday night at the Continental Club."

"What's that?"

"Oh, it's a great place. It's a really historic venue, near where I live on South Congress. They say that Elvis Presley played there in the fifties, but I don't know if it's true. Anyway, it's appropriate, because Corey and his friends often performed there."

"Sounds ideal."

"Yes, and what's more, it sold out in no time, so we've added an extra show on the Sunday. And do you want me to tell you something exciting?" asked Lucy.

"Of course."

"For the Sunday show, the Grams are re-forming."

This news took Ben a few moments to assimilate. How could the Grams reform without Corey Zander? But of course, lots of bands reunite without one or other original member. How had this come about?

"Well, we asked the Wilson brothers if they could contact the ex-members. They're all still there in the Tahlequah area and they were all up for it. And guess who's going to be Corey?"

"Bruce Springsteen? Prince?" joked Ben.

"Nearly. We've got Chuck Prophet to do it."

This was incredible news. The ex-Green On Red guitarist was the perfect choice, being a near contemporary of Corey, and performing similar music. The whole thing, added Lucy, was being done on a wing and a prayer and one rehearsal, but MP3s had been exchanged and arrangements learnt. For the remaining three Grams, this would be the first time they had played together in nearly a quarter of a century.

In the afternoon, Lucy had another treat for Ben. "We're going to be spending the next few days indoors in sweaty venues," she told him, "so now we're going for some fresh air and healthy activity." By this, she meant Zilker Park, a beautiful green open space near the Colorado River, Austin's "lung". First, they strolled among the trees by the river. Healthy looking youngsters (mainly students from Texas University, said Lucy) jogged past in all the requisite gear, while below them, rowing eights glided along the river, cutting symmetrical oar holes in the water. Then Lucy led him up the hill, with the promise of a surprise suitable for little boys. This was the Zilker Zephyr, a pleasure train which chugged around the park for a mile or so. Ben closed his eyes as the lonesome whistle rang out. Yes, he did feel like a child again.

The mystery of why Lucy had emailed him in Winchester a few days earlier, asking him to bring swimming gear with him, was now solved. Swimming trunks for a rock festival? Not exactly. Their destination was Barton Springs, a gorgeous, refreshing freshwater swimming pool carved into the rocks at the edge of the park. As Ben struggled to get into his trunks under a towel, Lucy had already peeled off her dress to reveal a green bikini and had dived into the water.

The shock as Ben joined her, somewhat more cautiously, was electric. In the blazing sunshine, the water was icy cold, initially agonising, then bracing, then fantastically invigorating as they swam up and down, occasionally stopping to splash each other like children.

Ben's lily-white body stood out a mile among the cool youngsters who populated the neat grass lawns surrounding the pool. The men were all muscular and covered with arty looking tattoos, as were most of the filmstar-like girls. Almost all of them were in clinches and most of them seemed to have a joint on the go. This was absolutely not the image Ben had had of Texas, but he had already read that Austin was not at all representative of the state. It was a pleasingly anachronistic oasis of liberalism in the middle of a desert of Republicanism.

As they lay on the bank in the sun, discussing the days ahead, Lucy leant towards Ben, her long hair brushing his face. She put her hand to his cheek.

"Is that cold?"

"Yes, but I like it."

He'd sort of known it was coming, but nonetheless his body shivered with excitement as she gently kissed him. He could have pulled away, protesting that he was engaged, but instead, he responded. He'd never felt like this before and was entirely in her power. The intensity increased over the next few minutes as they explored each other's bodies under the conveniently placed towel, until Lucy pulled back, looking at Ben's face intently.

"Bloody hell," said Ben.

"Don't worry, Ben," smiled Lucy. "Just relax. What happens in Austin stays in Austin."

They dined on blissful fajitas at a Mexican restaurant called "Gueros", nearly opposite Lucy's house on South Congress. Ben was agonizing a little about whether he should tell her that he couldn't get romantically involved when he was about to marry someone else, but Lucy bought him two Margaritas. So potent were these hallucinogenic cocktails that he just sat back in a haze of happiness and abandoned himself to the moment.

"I know what you're thinking, Ben, but you shouldn't worry. We're only having fun and nobody's getting hurt."

She dropped him back at the Super Eight at midnight, promising him the breakfast of his life. And so it was. At 10 the next day, she took him out to an organic diner on the highway called Star Seeds, where they feasted on a vegetarian breakfast and drank gallons of "free top-up" coffee.

"We call it 'bottomless'," explained Lucy. "Anyway, that's enough relaxing for now. The shows kick off today, so we have work to do."

Work on that first festival day, for Ben, wasn't too onerous. His job was to stand on the corner of Sixth Street and Red River, near the "Emo's All Stars" venue, and hand out flyers advertising the Corey Zander tribute concert at the Continental. There were some tickets left for the second show. Not everyone knew it had been added and it was important that it should sell out.

The street corner was an ideal spot for Ben to get a feel of how the festival worked. Consulting his programme, he saw that the "official" events started in the early evening and went on until 1 am. These were often record company "showcases" and featured some surprisingly big stars playing in little venues. During the day, however, there were also hundreds of unofficial shows going on which you could only find out about through the grapevine, on the internet or from posters and flyers. These were filled with hundreds of bands, in Austin partly to socialize, and partly with the dream of being "discovered", increasingly unlikely in the modern music industry. Basically, it was a massive four-day party accompanied by deafening music.

As he handed out his flyers, Ben made friend after friend. It was so unlike the drab, unfriendly UK. Within hours, he'd exchanged phone and email details with several people and found out about various "secret showcase" gigs. He'd also been told about good restaurants and got advice about the best local beers to drink. Priority number one, for him, was to get himself into tonight's show at Stubbs' Barbecue, yards from where he was standing, where the Pretenders were headlining.

Lucy had said she would be busy all day, so Ben was free to do what he wanted. Warned by new friends, he knew that the queues, or "lines", to get into Stubbs' would be huge, and that his Platinum Badge would not necessarily give him priority over other badge and wristband holders. So he lined up outside the fence at 6 o'clock. Already one of the support bands acts could be heard striking up inside. It was a young UK band called Broken Links.

He'd done the right thing. By 7.30, he was in and had negotiated his way to the very front. It wasn't easy, as the whole site, one of Austin's few outdoor venues, was on a slope and covered in rubble, rocks and steps. He spotted James Walbourne, the Pretenders' lead guitarist, in the wings. He'd once met James at the Windmill venue in Brixton, London, and was tempted to call out to him, but realized with an inward smile that people like James must meet hundreds of people and certainly wouldn't recognize him. As the other support acts played, Ben (with the help of a few Lone Star beers and the odd tequila) felt warmer and warmer, surrounded by, nay, squashed together with scores of like-minded music lovers.

At 10 o'clock on the dot, the Pretenders hit the stage, the blue stage lights emphasizing Chrissie Hynde's features and the rock poses of the guitarists. Drummer Martin Chambers, as usual, was surrounded by huge plexiglass screens. It was a special showcase occasion, so there was none of that dreaded "here's a new song" stuff, but an uninterrupted flow of Greatest Hits. "I Go To Sleep" gave Ben goose-pimples and by the time the band climaxed with "Brass In Pocket", Ben was hoarse from cheering and shouting for more. But a strict timetable was in place and there was to be no encore.

Thursday was a day for Lucy and Ben to spend together. There were special shows going on that Ben would never have heard about if he hadn't had Lucy's inside information. At a sweaty dive called "Headhunters" on Red River, a record label showcase for Canadian bands was in full swing, accompanied by free tacos and tequila. Ben had never heard of any of the artists, but loved them all. Then, the two of them took a bumpy bike rickshaw ride out to the edge of town, where, in a roadhouse-type venue called the Mean Eyed Cat, a party was being thrown by the UK magazine Mojo. Bands that would have cost a lot of money to see in the UK, such as Field Music, the Vaccines and the Jim Jones Revue, were playing here for free, inches away from them, through a decrepit, crackly PA. It was hard to describe the excitement. Ben was desperate to text people at home, describing his feelings, but he knew no one would understand. By his side all day, gently holding his hand as it were the most natural thing to do, was Lucy.

In the evening, they went to a billiard hall in town called Buffalo Billiards. In downtown Austin, at SXSW time, virtually every shop and bar turned itself into an impromptu music venue. The cacophony as they pushed their way through the milling crowds on Sixth Street was like a musical Tower of Babel, amplified sounds coming from all directions and colliding in the middle of the street. Buffalo Billiards was rammed because the occasion was a Texas showcase, featuring Centro-Matic and Slobberbone, both from nearby Denton, and headliners Midlake, a band now also popular in Europe. Here, Ben and Lucy handed out the last of their flyers. Their job was done, because Lucy received an email on her phone to confirm that both shows had now sold out. Most shows at SXSW were not pre-bookable and admission was free to badge holders, but an exception had been made for these ones, as they were charity events in aid of the newly founded Corey Zander Foundation. The brainchild of Lucy, this was to subsidize educational activities for the children of musicians.

On Friday, Ben and Lucy had to meet early. A rehearsal was to take place at a bar called Jovita's. Showcase events were due to take place there from 1 pm, so the rehearsal had been set for an ungodly 9 am. Chuck Prophet, himself due to play at Jovita's that afternoon, was a renowned teetotaller and by far the most alert person there. Ben found himself drinking ice cold Dos Equis beer at 10 o'clock in the morning, a feeling of delicious decadence.

Ben was formally introduced to Jesse, Mark and Will, the remaining members of the Grams.

"We couldn't believe it when we heard the news. It's so incredibly sad. It's just crazy. How the hell did it happen? Who did it, and why?"

"Well, we know who did it, but no one knows why. He was just a victim of random violence, an unfortunate person caught in the wrong place at the wrong time. The trial should take place sometime in April. None of it makes any sense, I'm afraid. My biggest fear is that the guy might get off on a technicality."

Once the rehearsal had got going, Ben and Lucy left. They didn't want to get in the way, and they didn't want to spoil the enjoyment of Sunday's show for themselves. The Oklahoma guys had prepared well and Chuck, taking Corey's role, was the consummate professional. So the two "lovebirds", as Jesse described them, causing both of them to blush and Ben to issue a flat denial, spent the day at yet another suburban bar, this time Maria's Taco Express. Here, local icon Alejandro Escovedo was holding his annual musical picnic, featuring a bewildering array of over a dozen bands that he'd met on his constant tours of the US and invited to Austin. The dapper Alejandro compèred the day in his bootlace tie, black suit and shiny winklepickers, while Lucy and Ben feasted on enchiladas and tried, unsuccessfully, to go easy on the iced Margaritas.

That evening was mind-blowing for Ben, as he and Lucy wangled their way into the tiny Cedar Street Courtyard for a "top secret" show by the Flaming Lips. As the confetti rained down and the balloons bounced, Ben found himself holding up the crouched figure of Wayne Coyne, as he rolled out over the crowd in his giant transparent pod. Then, he held Lucy tight as Coyne sang the saddest song ever written:

"Do you realize, that everyone you know one day will die?"

In view of tomorrow's planned event, it could scarcely have been more poignant, and both of them wept, their tears mingling among the falling kaleidoscope of floating paper.

Much of the following morning was spent at the Continental Club, preparing for the evening. Then, in the afternoon, Ben's Platinum Pass ensured that he was able to return to the Convention Center for Chrissie Hynde's keynote speech. She talked for 45 minutes on the topic of "Ethics in the Music Industry", likening some industry business practices to "people clubbing seals to death in order to make coats out of their skins". It wasn't what the assembled management types wanted to hear, and there were a few sharp intakes of breath. Ben found the entire thing spellbinding.

The Saturday line-up was chalked up on the blackboard behind the bar at the Continental: Freedy Johnson, Kimmie Rhodes, Jon Dee Graham, Amy Boone, Alejandro Escovedo, and the Resentments, the last being a supergroup of local musicians. Ben had to do an hour's shift on the door, but even from there, he didn't miss a minute of the music. The pattern was similar for most acts, and each of them played their normal set, interspersed with one or two Zander songs, and of course, memories and anecdotes, many of them referring affectionately to the trouble his weakness for the ladies could get him into. The mood, as had been the intention, was celebratory rather than sad.

Queues formed early on Sunday evening for the Grams reunion. It was the hottest ticket in town, and a large blackboard outside proclaimed "Sold Out – No Badges". This meant that scores of casual industry people who hadn't bought advance tickets were turned away. Ben's job was to tell people, "Sorry, you can't come in without a ticket". The irony wasn't lost on him. Only months before, he hadn't been able to give Corey Zander tickets away.

Two supports played before the Grams hit the stage. Chuck Prophet was by far the coolest-looking person in the band. Jesse and Mark both now spotted bushy beards and a few excess pounds, while drummer Will was completely bald. Chuck was clearly representing not the recent, unhealthy and overweight Zander, but the svelte, tight-trousered rocker of his youth. The preparation had paid off, as they blasted, to everyone's amazement, through a couple of ancient Chocs tracks, a few songs from Corey's solo career and an almost complete run through of the Grams' "Desert Grave" album. Truth to tell, Chuck Prophet was a far better guitarist then Corey had ever been. As they returned for a second encore, people in the crowd were shouting out for "Mad And Bad". "Sorry, we don't know that one," said Chuck into the microphone with a grin. "Ha, only kidding," he added, as, with a Townshend windmill, he crashed his Telecaster into the opening power chord. There wasn't a dry eye in the house. Any nonsense about a "Curse of Zander" certainly hadn't taken effect on this triumphant evening.

At the end, with condensation pouring down the walls, scores of people stayed behind to discuss the evening and swap memories, but Lucy took hold of Ben's hand.

"Tonight, you're coming home with me."

Ben hesitated.

"Don't worry, Ben," she laughed. "I won't make you sleep in Corey's bed. There's plenty of room in mine."

....

Ben woke before Lucy in the morning, his mind a buzzing storm of conflicting emotions. He turned his head to make sure it hadn't been a dream, but no, the blonde locks on the pillow confirmed the truth. Sleeping with Lucy had been like nothing he had ever experienced before, the lithe tenderness an amazing lesson to an inexperienced person like him. It was the sensual naturalness of it all had thrilled, amazed and consumed him. For a few minutes, he lay back and basked in the memory. Now he knew what an "afterglow" was. But just a few minutes later, familiar insecurities and feelings of guilt began to intrude. What he had just experienced contrasted so much with the businesslike formality of sex with Rosie. What had he done? Was it right? Was it wrong? Could he love two people at the same time? Maybe he didn't love Rosie after all. His feelings now for Lucy were quite overwhelming and he didn't know what to do.

"I know what you're thinking, I always do," came a voice from beside him. Lucy kissed him gently. "But I don't want you to think about it today. We have a very important job to do. We're going for a picnic."

As they drove out of the city, Ben felt as if he were in a Western film, as the roads became dustier and the landscape more empty. A sign said "Welcome To Texas Hill Country" as they approached Fredericksburg, an extraordinary town in which everything seemed to be German, including, surreally in this heat, a Christmas shop, complete with sleighs and Santas. A few miles further on, they entered Enchanted Rock National Park and eventually rounded a bend to gaze upon the rock itself, a huge pink mound which looked like a turtle.

As Lucy removed the picnic basket and another bag from the boot (or "trunk", as she charmingly called it), Ben was reading the display board, which gave details of the Enchanted Rock:

> *"Humans have visited here for over 11,000 years. The rock is a massive, granite exfoliation dome that rises 425 feet above ground. Tonkawa Indians believed that ghost fires flickered at the top and they heard weird creaking and groaning sounds, which geologists say resulted from the rocks heating by day and contracting in the night. A Conquistador, captured by the Tonkawa, described how he escaped by losing himself in the rock area, giving rise to an Indian legend of a 'pale man, swallowed by a rock and reborn as one of their own'. He explained that the rock wove spells. 'When I was swallowed by the rock, I joined the many spirits who enchant this place.'"*

Ben felt like moaning and groaning himself, as the couple struggled up the trail that led to the summit, the rock red hot beneath their feet. Lucy had made some vegetable wraps and they ate them and drank copious amounts of bottled water. Then she stood up, reaching into the other bag and pulling out her father's urn.

"I wanted you to be here for this, Ben. We're going to scatter his ashes."

"Why here?" asked Ben, although he already knew the answer.

"Because it's an enchanted place. I know the Native Americans who lived here weren't Choctaws, but I still felt Dad would feel at home here, among all the other spirits."

It certainly felt right, as the ashes blew in the breeze and settled among the scrub growing on the pink granite. The two of them closed their eyes for a moment.

"Goodbye Corey," said Lucy.

"Goodbye Corey," repeated Ben. "This is where you belong."

It was time for Ben to go home, although he didn't really know where home was. His eyes had been opened to another world, and his confusion was complete.

Chapter 11

Rosie took some time off work and collected Ben from Heathrow. This was preferable to the National Express coach, and gave them some time for conversation. Ben was tempted simply to confess all and declare the relationship over, but Lucy had made him promise to view the week as just an adventure. To see it as anything else would be unrealistic. Ben told Rosie a bit about the festival, but she wasn't that interested. She wanted to talk about the wedding. Good old Robert had agreed to fund a reception at Lainston House, wasn't that exciting?

Having mendaciously expressed his delight at the news, Ben asked about the murder case. It had been confirmed that the trial would begin on April 19. Rosie had opened a letter from the Crown Prosecution Service that had arrived addressed to Ben, in which he was requested to keep that week free, as he would be a witness. Rosie hadn't received an equivalent letter, so she assumed that she wouldn't be called. Robert, on the other hand, had.

They decided that it would be safe for Ben to stay over at Taplings Road for one night. They had a couple of drinks, some pleasant chat in anticipation of the wedding preparations, and eventually they slept together. It wasn't the same by any means, but the sensible part of Ben's brain was coming to terms with the feeling that Lucy had been right. It had simply been an adventure, a sideways step, and now he had to adjust back to normal life – or at least, as normal as it could be until the trial was over.

In the morning, Rosie dropped Ben off at Romsey Station, where he took the train back to Bradford-on-Avon. Over the coming weeks, she forwarded letters to him that contained details of what he should do to prepare for the trial. What it boiled down to was that he would need to present himself at Winchester Crown Court on Monday, 19th April at 9 am.

Ben drove over to Winchester on the Sunday, staying at Chilbolton Avenue and being treated to a Sunday roast, cooked by Diana. The four of them sat around in the evening, mainly discussing wedding details. Phil Clark, landlord of The Narrowboat, had said he would be delighted to be best man. As for the trial, there was little to talk about or prepare. As far as Robert and Ben were concerned, they could do no more or less than tell the truth. Unlike the defendant, they wouldn't have sleepless nights worrying about possible inconsistencies in a fake story.

On Monday morning, Ben and Robert walked down Romsey Road together, through the rush-hour traffic, arriving punctually at 8.55. Robert had had to book some days off school, a matter of some embarrassment. There was a procedure to get through security and identify themselves before entering the austere, wood-panelled witness room. There they sat for a couple of hours, uneasily avoiding the eyes of Dean Harris and Jason Bright, who were also there, both looking extremely uncomfortable in their suits and ties. Among other witnesses, Andy, the landlord of The Station, was also present, but nobody talked, other than asking bland questions about the whereabouts of the toilets or if anyone had change for the coffee machine. Meanwhile, the trial of Barry Mort was beginning.

....

The nervous members of the jury were shown to their seats. One or two of them were plainly already suffering from claustrophobia, squeezed onto the wooden benches, fiddling with their pencils and anxiously chewing their lips. None of them had asked to be there and none of them wanted to be there, forced to take days off work which they could ill afford. Each and every one of them, as they parted from their families that morning, had wished, "Oh God, let's hope it isn't a murder."

The judge, Mr Justice Cecil Pocklington, entered, and then the defendant, Barry Mort, was brought into the dock. The members of the jury were sworn in, hands and voices shaking. Mort had scrubbed up and he, too, was wearing a tight-fitting suit with a dark tie. The clerk of the court read out the murder charge and Mort was invited to plead. There was no sign of aggression or resentment in his manner as he looked straight ahead and said "Not Guilty".

It was now time for the prosecuting counsel, Nigel Debrett, to make his initial submission. "Ladies and gentlemen of the jury, the incident you will hear described is a disturbing case of mindless violence and a salutary lesson to us all on the dangers of alcohol misuse. You will hear how an entirely innocent man was abused and eventually killed by a complete stranger, someone who didn't even know him.

"Some of you may have heard of the victim, Mr Corey Zander. Mr Zander was a musician, a visitor to this country. On October 14th of last year, he was playing a concert at The Station, which is a so-called 'music venue' in Winchester. The simple facts of the case are as follows: towards the end of Mr Zander's performance, the defendant, Mr Mort, entered the hall and, for no good reason, started shouting abuse at Mr Zander. Understandably, the victim was distressed by this and did his best to ensure that the defendant desisted from that behaviour. During that process he may, quite justifiably, have behaved in a threatening manner towards the defendant. In any event, the defendant, who was seen by several witnesses to have been both drunk and aggressive, followed Mr Zander out of the room, threatening to kill him. This is where you, as the jury, will have to decide, based on the evidence you will hear, whether the defendant proceeded to murder Mr Zander, because the bare fact is that Mr Zander was discovered the next day, dead behind a rubbish container in the car park. He had been hit on the head by a brick, which was subsequently identified as the murder weapon.

"During this trial, you will no doubt be offered various possible explanations other than the obvious one. Firstly, you may be asked to believe that the defendant, Mr Mort, was acting in self-defence. We will show that, in fact, Mr Zander had long since left the room and posed no further threat to him. Or possibly, it will be suggested that he should be convicted of the lesser charge of manslaughter, or that the death was some kind of accident. On the contrary, the submission of the prosecution is that Corey Zander was the victim of cold-blooded murder, and that the perpetrator was the defendant, Barry Mort."

Both judge and jury were jotting notes as Debrett spoke.

After a few procedural comments from the judge, it was time to call the first witness, who was Andy Marriott, the Station's landlord.

"Is your establishment a place where violence often occurs?" asked Debrett.

"Not at all, sir. We have a policy of zero tolerance towards any sort of antisocial behaviour."

"Am I right in saying that Mr Mort, under the Winchester Pub Watch scheme, is banned from all city centre pubs?"

"That's correct, but he was already very drunk when he arrived, and also, he had shaved his head since the photo we were supplied with was taken. Unfortunately, we only have door security at weekends, and this was a Monday."

"Did you witness the event in the music room?"

"No, sir, I was serving in the front bar. I was aware that Mort and his friends had entered the building but most of the time they were in the beer garden and not causing any trouble."

"So what exactly did you see?"

"I saw Barry Mort running back into the music room. I talked to my assistant about what to do, but within a few minutes, Corey Zander came charging out of the room and into the car park. Then, a couple of minutes after that, Barry Mort comes out, shouting and swearing."

"What exactly was he saying?"

"Do you want the exact words?"

"Please".

"He was shouting 'fucking Yank cunt".

There was a brief murmur around the court and some of the jurors shuffled in their seats.

"What happened then?"

"He disappeared outside, and I don't know what happened there."

"Thank you, Mr Marriott."

Hylton was on his feet immediately.

"Mr Marriott, it is of no interest to the jury whether or not Mr Mort was subject to a banning order. You must only deal with the facts of the case. So, Mr Marriott, can you simply tell us – yes or no, please - whether you saw Mr Mort assaulting Mr Zander?"

"I didn't see it, no."

"Thank you. No further questions."

The judge looked up. "I think this would be a good moment for us to adjourn for lunch," he announced.

Ben suggested to Robert that they should walk up Romsey Road to the St James' Tavern, which did good sandwiches. As they walked across the cobbled courtyard, the public gallery had cleared, and a group of about ten friends and relatives of Barry Mort were standing in a huddle, lighting up cigarettes. As Ben and Robert passed, they turned and stared. Bright raised his middle finger to them in an act of defiance. "Careful what you say," called out Dean Harris. "You may regret it." Shelley, Mort's girlfriend, now with an extremely large bump, sneered at them and made a wanking gesture with her hand. For a frightening moment, Ben thought they were going to be followed, but no one moved.

In the afternoon, two members of the Bookworms and one of their friends were cross-examined. None of them were any help at all regarding the events in the room, as they had all been outside throughout Corey's set. The questioning hinged on what they had seen of events in the car park from the beer garden, where they had all been throughout Corey's set. They all described an identical scenario: Mort had come running up to his two mates, highly agitated, and had told them that they needed to get away, fast. Prior to that, they had seen Zander leaving the pub and disappearing into the car park. Had anyone else left the pub? Yes, but nobody had taken any notice of their faces or clothing.

Explaining the haste with which Mort and his friends had departed, all three witnesses replied, using almost identical words, that they would have been scared of Zander: "Have you seen him? He was big, and he'd already tried to strangle Baz."

It was late in the afternoon, so the judge said he thought it was an appropriate moment to adjourn.

We could all do with a cup of tea, mused Ben, as the announcement was made that they could go home. Spending a day in the witness room without actually being called had been a dispiriting experience. Ben had ploughed on through a Graham Hurley novel he was reading on his Kindle, increasingly troubled by the violent events in nearby Portsmouth that it contained, while Robert took the opportunity to catch up with some school admin on his laptop. The usher delivered a message saying that they could both reasonably expect to be called to give evidence the next day.

At the roundabout by the junction of Romsey Road and Chilbolton Avenue, they were about to turn right towards Robert's house, when they became aware, in the gathering twilight, that a small group of Mort's followers was striding up the road towards them. Uh-oh, thought Ben, this could be trouble.

"They're planning to intimidate us," said Ben.

"Why me?" pleaded Robert.

"Because you're a witness just as I am. What's more, your evidence is going to incriminate Mort even more than mine."

"They don't know that."

"They don't know anything, but they look like they mean business."

"Shall we run for it?"

"They don't know where you live, and they don't know I'm staying with you."

"Well, I'm going to run home. You do what you like."

In the months since the murder, Ben knew that Robert had had security fencing, automatic gates and CCTV installed, like many of his neighbours. On a whim, he darted left down Sleeper's Hill, leaving Robert to run off to the right towards his home. Instinct had told Ben they'd be after him and not Robert, and he seemed to be right. As he sprinted down the steep road, he could hear rapid footsteps following behind.

In his state of panic, Ben was aware of one lucid thought: Surely they weren't stupid enough to get themselves on a charge of intimidating a witness? But perhaps they were, and if that was the case, he was in danger of being seriously hurt. Their best mate was capable of murder, for goodness' sake, so he banished the fleeting thought that he had of stopping and trying to have a conversation with the gang. Turning left at the bottom of the hill, he leapt over a fence into the grounds of some student residences and hid behind a hedge, desperately trying to curb the loud, gasping breaths, brought on by terror and the unaccustomed physical activity.

His gamble paid off. He'd hoped they would assume that he'd carry straight on towards St Cross Road. He heard the footsteps of five people running on towards the main road. "Where's the cunt gone?" "Dunno, down here maybe?" It was twenty minutes before Ben dared to move a muscle. Maybe they weren't daft after all, and were silently waiting for him to emerge. Eventually, he trusted that he was safe for the time being. It was dark, so he couldn't be sure.

With his heart beating like a percussion orchestra, Ben tried to weigh up the options. He couldn't go to his flat, that was clear. Robert wouldn't thank him for leading them to his house, which they'd so far not targeted. With the desire to get right out of town now a top priority, Ben took out his iPhone and made an online booking for the Travelodge on the A34 at Sutton Scotney, then called a taxi and arranged to be taken there. Describing exactly where he was to a baffled switchboard lady, he figured he could probably leap into a taxi unscathed, even if the gang was still around.

They weren't, and Ben was able to spend a desolate evening watching TV in his box-like hotel room, dining on a fry-up in the Little Chef. He phoned Robert, who said that he hadn't been followed as far as he knew, thank goodness. Ben considered the idea of phoning the police and telling them what had happened, but of course the gang would deny it, and where was the evidence? He wondered what their motive had been anyway, eventually deciding it was probably just an unfocused desire for retribution on someone they blamed for their friend's predicament.

In the morning, Ben was first in the witness box. In one sense, he was terrified, because public speaking wasn't his forté. He'd seen enough courtroom dramas to know that he'd be in for a grilling and that the defence lawyer would try to make him look foolish and unreliable. On the other hand, he knew that all he could do would be to tell the truth, and nothing could change that. His voice trembled, his breathing became irregular, he felt dizzy and his hands sweated so much he feared he would drop the Bible. But he had to go through with it somehow.

For the prosecution, Nigel Debrett led Ben through a description of the evening's events, focusing on certain specific details.

"When Mr Mort first entered the room, why did you not prevent him from coming in?"

"Well, it happened so fast, and I wasn't expecting it. Everyone else just paid or showed a ticket, but he simply pushed his way in."

"How was he acting?"

"He was drunk and I was very intimidated by his behaviour. There were no security personnel I could have called on. I could have made a big thing out of it, but I didn't want to spoil the evening for everyone."

"Did he say why he was there?"

"Yes, he said his cousin was in the support band. That was one good thing, because I assumed he'd leave when they finished."

"And did he leave? Did he come back again later?"

"Yes, he did, while the main act was playing. That was a complete surprise. I wasn't even bothering to watch the door because I was listening to the music. I knew there'd been a bit of pushing and shoving between him and Corey in the front bar, so maybe that was the reason."

"So what happened when he re-entered?"

"The defendant started shouting abuse at Mr Zander. Eventually Corey got fed up with it and confronted Mr Mort." Ben stole a glance at Mort, impassive in the dock.

"Can you describe what happened next?"

"Well, there was a struggle. Corey had Mort up against the wall. For a moment, no one intervened because it was all such a shock."

"How did Mort react?"

"He tried to struggle, but Mr Zander was too strong for him. He was very angry at Mr Mort's behaviour and just went for him. But after a moment, he just let him drop, and stormed out." Ben wasn't looking at Mort now, aware that the next few questions would require him to make incriminating statements.

"So, when Zander left the room, what happened?"

"We tried to make sure Mr Mort was okay and he recovered within a couple of minutes. Then he left the room too, looking for Corey."

"Now think carefully, please, Mr Walker. What were Mort's precise words as he left?"

"He said, 'I'm going to fucking kill him'."

There was a brief ripple of whispering round the court. Some members of the jury looked at each other and made notes.

Debrett turned back to Ben.

"Am I right, Mr Walker, that you saw nothing of any events that then occurred outside?"

"That's correct."

"Why didn't you go outside yourself?"

"Well, I was relieved that Mort had gone and I wanted to clear up. I did wonder whether it might kick off outside, but I certainly didn't want to get involved."

"So, in summary, you have told us that Zander left the room and Mort followed him."

"Yes, sir, that is correct."

"Thank you, Mr Walker."

Damian Hylton, the defence lawyer, could hardly wait to get stuck in.

"Mr Walker, let's assume that your description was accurate. When you heard Mr Mort say 'I'm going to fucking kill him', do you seriously expect the jury to believe he was announcing to a roomful of people that he was about to commit a murder?"

"I believed that was in his mind, yes. He was out of control of what he was saying."

"Precisely. Out of control, and drunk, as you assert."

"Yes, I know drunk people sometimes say things they don't mean, but in this case, as I have said, Mort was very aggressive."

"In this court, we are only concerned with the facts, and not what you may or may not have believed at the time. Let's ask you something else. You are quite clear that there was a physical fight between Zander and Mort in that room, and that Zander was the aggressor?"

"Yes."

"So the DNA and fingerprints could both have come from the incident in the room and not from some alleged meeting later in the car park."

It was not a question, and Ben hesitated. He knew that this was the point at which Hylton would sense a lack of certainty in him and go on the attack.

"All I can say is that I did not see what happened in the car park." He took a deep breath. "But what I did see was this: Zander left the room and Mort followed him, making threatening remarks. Nobody can know exactly what happened after that because no one saw it."

"Precisely," said Hylton. "I have no further questions."

Next into the witness box was the pathologist, Dr Patel. The defence clearly wanted to put her on the spot about whether the wound could have been inflicted accidentally.

"We know that the car park was a depository for greasy fast food containers. It is quite feasible that Mr Zander might have slipped, is it not?"

"Yes."

"So if Mr Zander had slipped and fallen backwards, hitting his head on the brick, would that be consistent with the wound on the back of his head?"

"It's not out of the question."

Mr Debrett, for the prosecution, rose to his feet.

"What, in your expert opinion, is the most probable cause of this wound?"

"The most likely cause is being hit on the head with the brick." She nodded towards the weapon, wrapped in see-through polythene.

"But, if the victim, as is being suggested by the defence, had... er ... slipped," – Debrett smiled – "it would also have been possible for the wound to be inflicted in that way."

"It is feasible, but, in my opinion, unlikely. Zander was a large man, and if his head had hit the brick with force as he fell, it could have had a similar effect. In my opinion, it would be more likely that he had been pushed backwards, thus generating the force necessary to inflict the wound."

"So in effect, you are saying that Mr Zander was either hit on the head with a brick, or forcibly pushed over onto it?"

"Yes."

"Thank you, Dr Patel."

The final witness for the day was the Grams' fan, whose name turned out to be Richard Carswell. He'd been chosen out of several possible other audience members because he'd told the police that he'd be keen to give evidence.

"I saw the incident clearly, because Corey nearly tripped over my wife's leg as he left the stage. I turned round and watched as he headed straight for the guy who was shouting. He grabbed him by the neck but he dropped him almost immediately. Then he walked out, and shortly afterwards, Mort followed."

"What were the defendant's words as he left the room in pursuit of Mr Zander?"

"He said he was going to kill him." Again, whispers reverberated round the room.

Counsel for the defence, Mr Hylton, wanted to pursue this, but Carswell was having none of it.

"Don't we all often say things in the heat of the moment that we don't mean?"

"Yes, we do, but in this case, I am convinced that he meant it." Despite being repeatedly requested to stick to the facts, Carswell, Corey's greatest fan, was determined to express his opinion.

The judge looked up over his half moon glasses. "I think this would be an opportune moment to adjourn proceedings for the day." The jury was getting used to this by now. They fervently hoped there would be only one more day's evidence, as, to most of them, it was already an open and shut case, and all they wanted to do was go home.

Ben had planned his exit carefully. At lunchtime, he'd stayed in the witness room and eaten a sandwich purchased earlier from Sutton Scotney Services. Now, he jogged down to where he'd just phoned for a taxi to pick him up by the Elizabeth Frink horse statue in Upper High Street. The gaggle who he'd suspected of following him the previous day were just lighting up their cigarettes in the drizzle by the time Ben was gone. He was beginning to feel a lot like Alan Partridge as he settled down for his second night in the Travelodge.

Chapter 12

Robert Leighton was not impressed that he had had to spend another entire day in the witness room without being called, even though the usher patiently explained that there was no way anyone could tell how long cross-examination would last. Robert didn't like missing school and dreaded what might appear in Friday's "Weekly News".

He had to wait just a bit longer, as Wednesday's first witness was DCI Robin Bird. The police weren't prominent witnesses in this trial, simply because they hadn't been present at the time of the offence, only being called in nearly a day after it had happened. Bird's rôle was to confirm the details of the DNA and fingerprint evidence, and to go through the various witness statements that had been gathered at North Walls.

Damian Hylton had his knuckles severely rapped when he tried to bring up the fact that Ben Walker's fingerprint had also been found on the Grams badge. "You know as well as I do," admonished Mr Justice Pocklington, "that it is Mr Mort on trial here and no one else. Please do not bring up irrelevant matters." He turned to the jury. "I would like you to strike what you have just heard from your minds." Nevertheless, one or two jury members exchanged surprised glances.

It was 11 o'clock by the time Robert was sworn in. The jury didn't know it, but as far as the police were concerned, Robert was the pivotal witness. DCI Bird had warned him that defence counsel would do everything he could to discredit him. First to examine Robert, for the prosecution, was Nigel Debrett. He took Robert rapidly through the events in the room, but wanted more detail about what he had seen on leaving.

"What was your intention on leaving?"

"To go home. I set off up St Paul's Hill towards Oram's Arbour. But then it struck me that there was the potential for a violent scene. As long as I wasn't involved, I thought I could observe it from a distance. So I tiptoed back to the gateway at Pickfords, on the other side of the road."

"Why would you want to do that?"

"Because from there, I had a good view. If anything unpleasant happened, I could have immediately called the police on my mobile phone. I felt it was my duty."

"And did anything happen?"

"Not really. The students and some of Mr Mort's friends were in the beer garden, and Mr Zander had disappeared."

"So did you see Mr Mort at all?"

"Well, yes, I did, just for a moment. He came running out of the side door and into the car park."

"This is very important, Mr Leighton. Are you saying that Mr Mort didn't immediately run into the beer garden, but first went into the car park?"

"Yes, that's right."

"Do you know whether Mr Mort encountered Mr Zander in the car park?"

"That I don't know, but I did see two people arguing there."

"Really? Two people arguing? And who might those two people have been?"

"I'm afraid I can't say with certainty who they were. I could see two figures in the shadows. There was a light by the door, but the bulb wasn't very strong."

"Can you describe the two figures?"

"One was very large and the other was tall, but slimmer."

"And they were arguing, you say?"

"Yes, their voices were raised."

"Did you recognize either of the voices?"

"No, sir, not with certainty. I was too far away."

"You didn't hear any of the words they were saying?"

"No, sir."

"What happened then?"

"The figures disappeared into the car park and it went quiet."

"Did you see either of them again?"

"Yes, I did. After a minute or so, just as I was going to leave, Mr Mort came running out of the car park, collected his two friends from the beer garden and they all ran off towards the railway station."

"How did you feel about that?"

"I felt relieved because it meant that the incident was over and that Ben Walker wouldn't be in any more danger. I wouldn't have to call the police. That was a relief for me. Remember that Mr Walker was a member of my staff and any involvement with the police would have been very bad for the image of my school."

Now it was Mr Hylton's turn, for the defence.

"Now, Mr Leighton," he began, pretending to look baffled. "I take it you are not in the habit of frequenting – er – music venues such as The Station?"

"No, sir."

"And do you share Mr Walker's predilection for … he consulted his notes … "– er – 'Americana' music?"

"No, sir, I don't."

"So what on earth were you doing there?" His wig twitched with self-satisfaction.

"Well, Mr Walker is my daughter's fiancé, and he asked me to come along. I wanted to show support, especially because he told me that he hadn't sold many tickets."

"And I understand that your daughter had already gone home before any of the evening's significant events occurred?"

"That's right, she had a headache."

"Having listened to Mr Zander's music, I'm not surprised," responded Hylton with a smug grin.

"Stick to the point, please, Mr Hylton," intervened Mr Justice Pocklington, wearily.

"I apologize, my Lord. But it's still a mystery why you didn't accompany your daughter when she left, as she was feeling unwell."

"I would have liked to, but I'd been temporarily put in charge of the merch table while Mr Zander was on stage."

"Merch?"

"Merchandise, sir, CDs and badges. We didn't want anything to be stolen."

"No doubt. Please will you describe the events as they unfolded when the defendant entered the room for the second time."

Robert's description tallied exactly with what he had said before and, indeed, with everybody else's evidence.

"Now we come to the moment when you decided to leave the room. Why exactly did you decide to leave?"

"It was a combination of things. Firstly, I was tired, and there was nothing else I could usefully do. But more importantly, it had already turned ugly and I feared it might get worse. It was vital that I wasn't associated with anything that could bring my name into disrepute."

"Because of your reputation as a head teacher?"

"Exactly."

"So you decided, as it were, to 'run for it'?"

"If you want to put it like that, yes. Not wanting to get involved in a brawl is nothing to be ashamed of."

"Indeed. So if we are to believe you, you then lurked around so that you could observe events from a distance."

"I wouldn't call it lurking, but yes, that's what I decided to do."

"And it was at this point that you saw" – he consulted his notes – "or thought you saw, two shadowy figures arguing in the car park. Do you have the slightest idea who those two figures were?"

"I assumed they were Mort and Zander."

"That's a very big assumption, if I may say so. On what grounds did you come to that conclusion?"

"It just seemed obvious. Mort had just come out of the door and I knew that Zander was angry with him. I don't think it was an unreasonable assumption to make. Why should two completely random people be arguing when it was obvious that Mort and Zander had had an altercation just a few minutes before?"

"Your point is noted," said Hylton, "but it is up to the jury to decide whether your evidence is pertinent to the case."

With that, he swished his gown and sat down.

The court then adjourned for the day. Ben, still at Sutton Scotney Travelodge and OD-ing on daytime TV, would have loved an update on proceedings, but it had been made clear that there was to be no communication between witnesses once their evidence had been given, so he was left to stew.

....

On Thursday morning, it was time for the defence case to begin. As is the legal custom, the accused, Barry Mort, was the first person to be questioned for the defence, but first, Mort's counsel, Damian Hylton, made his introductory remarks.

"Members of the jury, the picture I will paint for you is quite a different one from that given by the prosecution. Whilst it is true that violence flared on the evening in question, we will show that, far from being perpetrated by the defendant, it was inflicted upon him. He does not deny that he may have said things which offended the victim, but is not a crime to offend someone. It is our submission that Barry Mort merely entered the room, shouted a few offensive words and then was attacked, in a most brutal manner, by Mr Zander, who came close to committing murder himself. The defendant was naturally frightened and fled the scene to avoid further trouble. Prosecuting counsel is quite wrong to predict that we will be asking you to consider self-defence or a lesser charge of manslaughter. The defence case is that Mr Mort is completely innocent and that the case against him should be dismissed."

Throughout the proceedings, Mort remained quietly defiant and completely confident in everything he said. First, he was questioned by his own counsel.

"Mr Mort, we have repeatedly heard that you were drunk when you entered The Station."

"I am not denying that, sir. I told the police from the start that I regret that. I'm aware that I have anger management issues when I take alcohol. That's why I have almost given up drinking, as my mentor will tell you."

"So why were you drunk on this occasion?"

"It was a one-off, because I'd won some money on the horses. I wish it hadn't happened."

"How do you feel about this case?"

"I feel I am the innocent victim, sir. I know I caused trouble, and I apologize for that. But that American tried to kill me, and now it's me in the dock."

"But it is alleged you threatened to kill him..."

"It was just the drink talking, sir. Of course I didn't mean it, I couldn't kill anyone."

"So how do you explain what has been described as an argument in the car park?"

"I dunno. I didn't hear no argument and I didn't have no argument. I just wanted to get away."

"Did you pick up a brick?"

"No, sir."

"Your fingerprints were not found on the brick."

"Exactly. So I couldn't have picked it up."

"Were you wearing gloves that evening?"

"I've never worn gloves in my life. I'm not a woman. You can ask anyone if I was wearing gloves and they'll tell you I wasn't."

"Did you have a pair of gloves in your pocket?"

"I could have, but I didn't."

"Thank you, Mr Mort."

This was the stage of the trial which should decide the jury's verdict. Mr Debrett hoped he hadn't met his match, but it was clear from the start that Mort wasn't scared of the prosecuting counsel, and wasn't going to be intimidated.

"If you've given up drinking, how is it that the police described finding empty cider cans around your house?"

"Shelley has a couple now and then. I have one or two a week. We have friends round. And I don't clean up very often." He held the lawyer's gaze.

"Does your partner drink while pregnant?"

"Keep to the point," interjected the judge .

"Do you have any kind of explanation for your appalling behaviour on that Monday evening? I assume you aren't denying what every single witness has described?"

"No, sir, I behaved very badly." Mort had been excellently schooled in refraining from swearing or flying off the handle. "For some reason, I took a dislike to the American."

"Did that justify you shouting and swearing at him?"

"No, sir, I am very sorry about that, but I didn't kill him."

"All in good time, Mr Mort. Do you think Mr Zander was justified in attacking you?"

"No, he wasn't. I was only having a bit of fun, and then he went for me."

"Did you encounter Mr Zander in the car park?

"No, sir, I did not."

"Did the two of you argue?"

"No, sir."

"Did you hit him with the brick?"

"No, sir."

"If you didn't hit him, did you push him over?"

"No, sir."

"Did you put on some gloves you had in your pocket, so that there would be no fingerprints?"

Mort remained steadfast. "No, sir, I did not do any of those things. I didn't see him or speak to him in the car park. I definitely didn't put on any gloves because I don't own any. The police searched my house and didn't find nothing. All I did was, I ran out, collected my friends and we left."

Mr Debrett continued. "Moving on, why did you say, 'Let's get the fuck out of here'?"

"How often do I have to tell you? I was scared."

"I put it to you that you said those words because you had just killed Mr Zander and it was essential to get away."

"No, sir, that is not true."

"So how do you explain the witness who saw you arguing in the car park?"

"He saw someone arguing. He didn't see me. He couldn't have, because I didn't have no argument."

The other main witnesses for the defence were Mort's friends Dean and Jason. First up was Dean Harris, who gave a performance which showed all the signs of having been rehearsed. Confirming that he hadn't even entered the music room after the support band had finished playing, he was in and out of the witness box in minutes. He told the defence counsel he'd spent the evening in the beer garden chatting with the students. Towards the end of the evening, Mort had gone back into the venue and, shortly afterwards, had come running out again.

Debrett wanted to pursue this.

"What did Mort say?"

"He said, 'Let's get the fuck out of here', so we all followed him."

"Why do you think he said that?"

"Because he was scared of that big American bloke."

"I put it to you, Mr Harris, that there could be another reason. Could it not be that Mort had done something to the American and wanted to get away fast before it was discovered?"

"No, sir, I don't think so."

"And did you hear the sound of an argument coming from the car park?"

Harris looked amazed. "No sir. I didn't hear a thing."

As far as Debrett was concerned, Jason Bright, next into the witness box, was the one to go for. He'd been briefed by the police that Bright was a misnomer, and that if anyone was going to fail to toe the party line, it would be him. Unsurprisingly, he successfully negotiated the soft questions asked by Hylton, but now it was the prosecutor's turn.

"So you're a smoker, Mr Bright?"

"Yes, why?"

"I was just wondering why you spent all that time outside in the cold, when you could have carried on playing on the quiz machine indoors."

"I was talking to me mates. There's no law against that." He was getting irritated already.

"Now, do you recall that, at the end of the evening, Mr Mort came running up to you, shouting 'Let's get the fuck out of here'?"

"Yes, I do."

"Was that before or after Mr Mort had had the argument in the car park?"

"It was after, of course."

"Ah, so you heard the argument?"

People started shuffling all round the court room.

"Yeah... No... Yeah... Well, what I mean is..."

"Be very careful, Mr Bright. Remember you are under oath. Did you, or did you not hear Mr Mort having an argument before you all ran away?"

Jason Bright was now sweating and shaking, trying to avoid the eye of Mort, who was staring at him in fury.

"Well, I sort of did, I'm not sure really, maybe I did, I can't remember clearly."

"Was Mr Mort running from the pub door or from the car park?"

"I don't know, I couldn't see, it all happened so quickly."

"Surely you remember something as simple as that?"

"No, er, I'd had a few drinks ..., no, I don't remember, I'm sorry."

Debrett turned and cast a brief, significant glance at the jury.

"Thank you, Mr Bright."

The final few minutes were taken up by a character witness for Mort, called by his defence lawyer. It was the "anger management mentor" who'd been looking after him. He described the good progress that Mort had been making.

"He is aware that he has had issues in the past, but he is determined to address them, especially in view of the fact that, within weeks, he will become a father for the first time."

"So you are describing a man who has overcome his problems and will shortly have a young baby to look after?"

"Yes, sir."

Now, at last, it was time for the closing speeches by the two counsel, followed by the judge's summing up and legal directions to the jury. Mr Debrett, for the prosecution, took the jury through the events for a weary last time.

"It boils down to whether you believe that Mr Mort had sufficient reason and was in the kind of mood that would allow him to commit murder. The evidence is quite clearly there before you, the DNA and fingerprints which could have come from the altercation in the pub but could equally well have come from the car park. Mr Mort denies ever being in the car park, but we have two witnesses, Mr Leighton, and, crucially, Mort's own friend Mr Bright, who describe seeing two figures arguing in the car park at the crucial moment in this case. And most important of all, everybody, including the defendant, agrees that Mort said he was going to kill Mr Zander. If you believe that is what he did, you must come to a verdict of Guilty."

Hylton's summing up was a tour de force of self-righteousness. "Members of the jury, the case effectively hinges on whether Mr Leighton and Mr Bright saw Mort and Zander arguing in the car park. Mr Bright is not absolutely sure what he saw, and as for the words used by Mr Leighton, well, they speak for themselves: 'assumed', 'obvious', 'thought'. None of these words add up to any concrete evidence at all. It could easily have been two completely different people arguing in that car park. No, members of the jury, you have before you a man of clear conscience. He has been candid about his failings, but he is shortly to be a father and has changed his ways. I am not going to ask you to consider a lesser verdict of manslaughter. For that, it would be necessary for Mr Mort to admit that he killed Mr Zander. He admits to no such thing. Mr Mort is completely innocent and for that reason, if you agree with me, you must pronounce him Not Guilty."

There was now an adjournment to allow the judge to prepare his final summing-up. When the jury filed back in, he addressed his remarks directly to them.

"We have here a very sad case. A visitor to our shores has lost his life in tragic circumstances. Your job now, having heard the evidence, is to decide whether or not to convict Barry Mort of his murder. Remember, please, that you can only convict if you are absolutely certain that he killed Mr Zander, and that he intended to so. What makes your task harder is the fact that there were no eyewitnesses to the killing.

"Let us first examine the forensic evidence. It has not been challenged by the defence that the object which killed Mr Zander was a brick that was lying in the car park, normally used to prop the door open. This brick has hundreds of fingerprints on it but – and you may consider this important – neither the fingerprints nor the DNA of Mr Mort. The prosecution's case is that there is a simple explanation for this, namely that Mr Mort was wearing gloves. They say this could also explain why there is no forensic evidence linking Mr Mort to the handle of the rubbish container. However, Mr Mort quite clearly and explicitly denies wearing gloves on that day.

"Where there is evidence of Mr Mort's presence, however, is on Mr Zander's coat and, in particular, on a badge he was wearing. There are fibres from Mr Mort's jacket in evidence, as well as an unmistakable fingerprint on the badge. Your job, members of the jury, is to decide whether the prosecution have proved the case against him so you are sure about it. During the trial, three opportunities have been put forward for this evidence to have got there: firstly, when the two men brushed past each other in the doorway; secondly, as they scuffled in the music room; and thirdly, that they argued and fought again in the car park.

"That is the next thing you have to decide. We have one witness, Mr Leighton, who saw two figures arguing, but cannot say with 100 percent certainty that those figures were Mr Zander and Mr Mort. We have another witness, Mr Bright, who can't quite remember what he saw. He may or may not have seen the argument. You will have to decide whether the evidence from these two witnesses is reliable, because we have heard from several other witnesses, in particular Mr Harris, that there was no argument at all.

"Regarding the facts of the case, you will have to examine the timeline and decide whether Mr Mort, as he insists, came straight out of the room, collected his friends and ran away, or whether he first had an encounter with Zander in the car park.

"Now we come to the matter of a motive. The prosecution do not have to demonstrate a motive, and you should not speculate, but you are entitled to consider proper inferences that arise out of evidence you accept. Was the fact that he had been assaulted by Mr Zander sufficient motivation for Mr Mort to want to gain revenge? If so, how premeditated was his action? Did he decide to kill Mr Zander before picking up the brick, or was it in the rage of the moment? Or was it, indeed, an accident? I ask this because, contrary to what defence counsel has asserted, I direct that, in law, you will indeed have to consider the possibility of manslaughter. I shall return to this in a moment.

"You will have to consider how Mr Zander was killed. The first possibility is that Mr Mort came up behind him and hit him on the head with the brick. If you believe that, you will have to accept that the fingerprint on the badge, being on the front of Mr Zander's jacket, came from the earlier scuffle. Alternatively, Mort could have pushed Zander over backwards during the argument in the car park. That would certainly explain the fingerprint, but would Mort have had the physical strength to do that? Was he not so drunk that it would have been impossible? Either way, if you believe that is what happened, then you have no alternative but to convict Mr Mort of the lesser crime of manslaughter. But you must be sure that his death was not simply an accident, or may have been an accident. If it was an accident, the defendant must be found Not Guilty of any crime.

"Absolutely crucial in this case, you may think, members of the jury, are the words that Barry Mort used as he left the music room. He said, and nobody disputes this, 'I'm going to (expletive) kill him'. You might conclude that this was clear evidence of his intention, which he proceeded to carry out. Or was it, as he asserts, simply bravado, an empty threat with no meaning, the sort of thing we all say in the heat of the moment?

"When you retire, members of the jury, you will have to discuss the final possibility, which is that there was no murder or manslaughter at all. We have heard that it is not impossible that Mr Zander slipped on something on the floor and fell backwards onto the brick. That would tally with Mr Mort's assertion that there was indeed no argument in the car park.

"The fact remains that Mr Zander tragically died that night. Before you retire, I have to remind you once again that you can only find Mr Mort guilty of murder if you have absolutely no doubt that he killed Mr Zander and that he intended to do so, or to do him some grievous bodily harm. If you believe that he killed him by his deliberate actions, but without that intent, you must bring in a verdict of manslaughter. And if you are not sure in your own minds that the prosecution have proved either of these situations, then Mr Mort must be pronounced Not Guilty.

"Consider the murder charge first. If you are all agreed he is guilty of that, you should not consider manslaughter at all. It is only if you are agreed that he is not guilty of murder, that you can go on to consider the alternative charge of manslaughter. "

Chapter 13

None of the jurors had ever taken on such a duty before, so they listened attentively, if nervously, as a clerk gave them their instructions. It was a plain, neon-lit, white-painted room with a large table in the middle, surrounded by plastic chairs. There were the formalities of the organization of toilet breaks and how to work the coffee urn in the corner, but the most important thing to do immediately was to elect a foreman, who would act as chairperson of the group and later deliver the verdict. Luckily, a man in his thirties called Geoff Taylor volunteered straight away and was elected unopposed, the others being relieved they weren't going to have to take on the responsibility. Having pointed out the whiteboard on the wall and the felt tip pens to go with it, the clerk departed.

"Okay, so the first thing we need to do is introduce ourselves," said Geoff, taking charge in a businesslike manner. Among the twelve were a retired female teacher, a young fireman, a rather posh lady who described herself as a housewife and a very quiet librarian with a beard. Nobody seemed very confident or assertive as Geoff outlined how he thought they should proceed.

"It's possible we can deal with this quickly," he said. "Let's go round the table. Maybe we'll all agree and we can go home. So, bearing in mind what the judge says about being absolutely sure, who thinks Mort is guilty? I'll start. I say he is guilty."

This took the other jurors aback, as they hadn't expected to be put on the spot so soon.

"Hold on a minute," interjected the fireman, whose name was Guy, "don't you think we should have our discussion first?"

"We'll have a discussion, of course," replied Geoff. "This is just to establish where we all stand at the outset."

As each juror spoke, the main sentiment of all of them was that their instinct was that Mort was guilty, but not all of them had "absolutely no doubt". Seven members said immediately that they believed he was guilty, while five weren't sure.

"Okay, we have to try and reach a unanimous verdict, so what we have to do now is try to reach a point where we all agree. Could one of you explain why you aren't certain he's guilty?"

The retired schoolteacher's name was Dorothy Martin. Tentatively, she tried to put her feelings into words.

"My fear is that if we pronounce him guilty, he will go to prison for many years. He has a baby being born soon, and the mentor told us he was turning his life around. Doesn't someone like that deserve a second chance?"

"Not if he's a murderer, no," responded Geoff.

"No, of course not, but it's this 'absolutely certain' thing that makes me hesitate, because no one actually saw him do it."

"Look," said Geoff, "you only have to take one look at him to see he's a violent thug and a chav. I wouldn't be surprised to find out he's got a record as long as your arm."

Now the librarian, Brian Houghton, joined in. "That isn't relevant, though, is it? We were clearly told to stick to the facts of the case, without prejudice. We can't convict someone just because we don't like him; we have to have proof."

"That's how I feel too," agreed Dorothy.

"All right then." Geoff tried another tack. "Let's go through the facts as we know them and see where that leads us. Let's start with how Mort behaved in the music room, shouting and swearing for no reason. Surely that was beyond the pale?"

The posh lady, Andrea Hamilton, agreed. "Yes, quite appalling. In my opinion, the man was completely out of control. That proves that he was in the state where he could do anything."

"Even commit murder?"

"Yes, he was certainly drunk and angry enough, all the witnesses agreed on that."

It was noticeable that, round the table, there were some jurors who were determined to keep their heads down and not join in with the discussion. This was a mixture of shyness and lack of confidence. Several of them simply nodded in agreement with everything anyone said, indicating the indecision engendered by the ambivalent nature of the case: where was the concrete evidence?

"Let's discuss what we think actually happened in that car park then," suggested Geoff. Does anyone here think it was an accident?"

"No way was it an accident," said the fireman. "All that stuff about banana skins, who would ever believe that? He's just had a major row with someone and been threatened with murder, and all of a sudden he slips over and splits open his head." His voice was filled with sarcasm.

Dorothy wasn't convinced. "Nevertheless, we can't be sure it wasn't an accident. The pathologist said it was a possibility."

Mrs Hamilton disagreed. "No, it would be too much of a coincidence for him to have fallen over just at that moment. I believe that, at the very least, he must've been pushed."

No one apart from Dorothy thought that manslaughter was an option. They all agreed that, if a simple accident had occurred, the brick would have been still on the floor and wouldn't have been picked up and put in the bin. They were amazed that no one seemed to have pointed that out in court, and Dorothy was forced to concede the point.

The librarian, Brian, intervened at this point. "That's the crux of the matter, isn't it? The old chestnut 'Did he fall or was he pushed?' As a matter of interest, does anyone here think Mort simply bashed him over the head with a brick?"

"I do." It was Geoff again. "That's exactly the sort of thing a bloke like that would do."

"I think so as well," said Mrs Hamilton. "We know he threatened to kill him, so that's what he did, in my opinion."

"I take your point," accepted Dorothy. "But to what extent do we accept that it was a genuine murder threat? Several people, and even the judge, pointed out that it could have been just empty words, not really meaning anything."

"I'm quite clear in my mind," said Guy. "If you say you're going to kill someone and the next thing you know, the guy's been found dead, there's got to be a connection."

"On top of that, Mort's DNA and fingerprints are all over the body. What more proof do you want?" The foreman was clearly keen to get home to his dinner.

"I'm still not sure." This was Dorothy again. "If it was murder, he must have come up behind him and hit him. That means the fingerprint on the badge and the DNA on the jacket came from earlier. We could dismiss them as evidence altogether."

Guy wasn't convinced. "We need to consider what the witnesses said about what happened outside. It was obvious that they'd all rehearsed what they were going to say. Those students in the band would have been scared stiff of Mort and his gang and said anything they told them to. You know, 'You never saw a thing, get it? Otherwise you know what's going to happen to you.'"

Brian, the librarian, helped out. "Yes, this is the crucial thing for me, and it does make me think he's guilty. He's obviously put the frighteners on everyone to say they saw nothing. Where it went wrong was when the lawyer tricked Bright into saying he might have seen something. Did you see Mort's face? He wasn't expecting that."

Mrs Hamilton joined in. "More importantly, the only credible witness, who hadn't been nobbled, did actually see an argument going on in the car park."

"That's what I was going to say," agreed Guy. "That headteacher is the only impartial witness, so he's the one I believe."

Dorothy was weakening. "Was he completely impartial though? He was connected to that young man who put the concert on."

Geoff snorted: "So that's a reason to invent a story to get someone convicted of murder? I don't think so."

The jury had been deliberating for less than an hour and Geoff sensed that they could get the verdict settled rapidly.

"Let's just check round the table again. Raise your hand if you think he's guilty."

This time, eleven hands were raised, some more confidently than others. Peer pressure, which Dorothy Martin was well acquainted with from her work as a teacher, was fully operational. But she was not ready to give in yet.

"I'd like to remind everyone, before we sleepwalk into a verdict we may regret, that the judge said we could only convict if we had absolutely no doubt that he did it, and did it on purpose. Should we not at least consider the possibility of manslaughter, that he may have pushed Zander over and didn't intend to kill him?"

Geoff was impatient now, all pretence at impartiality discarded. "You know what? You're just a do-gooder. If we go down that path, we're literally letting someone get away with murder."

"Hang on," objected Brian, "there's no need to talk to her like that. We're all entitled to our opinions."

"Well," said Mrs Hamilton, "I've got my own opinion, thank you, and that is that Mort would never have had the strength to push over a huge man like Zander."

It went quiet for a moment before Dorothy, still not quite defeated, expressed her final doubts. "Don't forget that the head teacher didn't actually identify the people who were arguing. He said he couldn't see them clearly."

That did it. A chorus of disapproval swept the room. "Ridiculous"; "Oh, for goodness' sake"; "Who the hell else do you think it was?" Dorothy was in a minority of one.

"Okay, so what are we going to do?" asked Jeff. "We can carry on debating for a few more hours, until the judge lets us bring in a majority verdict. Or we can agree it's manslaughter" – heads shook all around him – "or Dorothy can admit she's barking up the wrong tree."

All eyes turned to Dorothy, who showed signs of confusion. She was an elderly lady, merely trying to "do the right thing," but in the face of total opposition, even she now doubted her instincts.

"Remember, Dorothy," said Brian, bringing the atmosphere down to a more gentle level, "you'd have to live with the responsibility of letting a guilty man get away with a vile crime. Would your conscience allow that?"

Dorothy swallowed. Then, tentatively, she raised her hand. "You're probably right. Maybe I'm being foolish. I'll go along with your decision."

"Excellent." Geoff's hand was already reaching for the bell to call the clerk of the court.

....

Minutes later, the jury filed back into court. The judge wasted little time, inviting the foreman to stand up.

"Have you reached a verdict?"

"Yes, your honour."

"Do you find Kevin Edward Mort guilty or not guilty of murder?"

"Guilty."

Pandemonium broke out instantly. Shelley burst into tears, a couple of family members stood up, pointing, gesticulating and shouting, while Mort himself simply stood in the dock, pale and open-mouthed, shaking his head. After order was restored, the judge asked for a brief adjournment while he considered the sentence. When he returned, he addressed his remarks directly to Mort, who still appeared completely shell-shocked, his eyes red from where he had apparently been crying.

"Mr Mort, you have been found guilty of murder and it is now my duty to pronounce sentence. In so doing, I have taken into account several mitigating matters. Firstly, I accept that you have been making efforts to overcome your criminal past. Secondly, I am aware that you are shortly to become a father, and thirdly, I accept that you were severely provoked. Nevertheless, murder is the most serious crime that can be committed. As you have been found guilty, it has been accepted that it was both cold-blooded and premeditated. Taking all these things into consideration, I sentence you to life imprisonment with a minimum term of fifteen years."

Shelley immediately collapsed again, while Mort looked for a second as if he was about to faint. The members of the press present scribbled their last notes and rushed off to file their stories. The BBC South reporter took up a position in front of the flint walls of the courthouse, ready to film a piece for South Today. The jurors, having filled in their expenses forms, drifted off to their cars, buses and trains, all feeling drained. The traditional huddle of friends and relatives lit up their cigarettes, looking as if they were at a funeral. Poor Kevin Bright, knowing how badly he had let the side down, was being comforted as he sobbed. Nobody seemed to be blaming him; they were all too shell-shocked. Things had happened so fast. Not even Derek White, the reporter from the Weekly News, had expected to be filing his report so soon. If he rushed, he could just hit the deadline before the paper went to print in a couple of hours' time. As he hurried back to the office, he was pleased that he'd prepared his report in advance. All that was missing was the verdict, and the little matter of Mort's chain of previous convictions for unprovoked acts of violence, released immediately after the sentence. This certainly comforted Dorothy and reinforced the rest of the jury in their confidence in the verdict. A bad guy had got what he deserved.

Chapter 14

Ben Walker and Robert Leighton had watched the verdict and sentence from the public gallery, ignoring the glares of the Mort gang. Now, even though no one showed any sign of chasing them this time, they quickened their step as they headed for the St James' Tavern for a celebratory drink. Ben called Rosie on her mobile. She'd just finished work and joined them. Well, they agreed, maybe there wasn't much to celebrate. The episode had been a dark one for all of them, putting them and their relationships under massive stress. Ben's career had been hampered and Robert's position compromised, but, worst of all, someone had died needlessly and someone else would now spend years in prison and be unable to watch his child grow up. Tomorrow, they all agreed, would mark what was so often called "the first day of the rest of their lives", when they could at last move on and start to make plans.

Derek White, meanwhile, filed his report in the nick of time.

> **GUILTY!**
>
> Fifteen years for the "brick murderer"
>
> Today, a brutal thug was put behind bars, found guilty of the cold-blooded murder of an innocent musician. A jury took just over an hour to deliver a unanimous guilty verdict on Barry Mort (31) of Stanmore, Winchester.
>
> In the most sensational murder case to hit Winchester for decades, Mort first abused and then attacked Corey Zander in the car park of The Station venue in St Paul's Hill, staving in his head with a brick. He found the weapon lying on the floor and used it to kill the well-known American musician (54), who had just performed a concert. Earlier, the two of them had clashed inside the venue, angering Mort. Zander's body was discovered the next day, clumsily hidden behind a rubbish container in the car park.

> After the verdict was pronounced, it was revealed that Mort had a string of previous convictions for violence. Teacher Ben Walker, who had invited Zander to perform in Winchester, and who at one point was himself under suspicion of the murder, was unavailable for comment last night. Find out more on our website www.hantsweeklynews.co.uk

....

On Saturday, Ben went round to Chilbolton Avenue. This was truly the calm after the storm, and he felt safe enough now to emerge from his hotel exile. He was thinking now of maybe returning to the flat in Weeke and starting again with Rosie. All through the trial, and indeed in the period leading up to it, he'd stayed in close touch with Lucy by email. He had suggested that she should think about coming over for the trial, but on balance, they agreed that there was little to be gained. Ben was relieved, because he was in enough emotional turmoil as it was without having to struggle with a bad conscience. But now he was able to deliver the good news.

"At least he got what he deserved," she emailed back. "Now we can both get on with our lives. It's been a difficult time but justice has been done. XOXO."

Over lunch, as wedding details were discussed, things seemed to have returned to something resembling normality. There were now only four weeks to go and masses of things needed to be arranged. In the afternoon, Ben and Rosie kept a long-planned appointment with the vicar of Littleton, as he talked them through how the ceremony would work. Ben had severe doubts about the church wedding, considering that neither of them were remotely religious, but Rosie had set her heart on it and it seemed churlish to deny her this pleasure.

On Sunday, Ben took the train back to Bradford-on-Avon, feeling much more comfortable about life. He did still think about Lucy a lot and occasionally felt slightly conscience-stricken about having been unfaithful to Rosie. The evening before, he'd had a bit too much to drink and found himself on the point of confessing all, but luckily managed to restrain himself. Some things in life are better left unsaid.

Life at The Narrowboat picked up where it had left off, with a few music nights already booked in. The alternative lifestyle was comfortable, but Ben knew it was unrealistic to expect it to continue. His parents were, of course, delighted at the verdict and said he could stay as long as he wanted, but Ben and Rosie had other plans.

One thing was clear to them. It would be impossible for them to stay in Winchester.

"I can't bear the thought of walking along Jewry street one day and bumping into Shelley, pushing her pram with Mort's baby in it," said Rosie.

"Maybe she wouldn't recognize you?"

"No, but she'd certainly know you. We wouldn't be able to go out together."

"Yeah, agreed Ben, "and having been chased once by Mort's mates, it's only a matter of time before they came after me again, and this time I might not be able to hide."

"We need to get away."

"Professionally, there's nothing left for me in Winchester. I'll never forget the eggs and the graffiti. That 'no smoke without fire' brigade will always be there."

So, after a lot of discussion, the couple concluded that the time had come for them to strike out on their own. They both loved the Bridport area of West Dorset, with its beautiful coastline and laid-back atmosphere, so the plan was to relocate there. It would be an ideal area to bring up children. It was a property hotspot, so Rosie was confident of getting work there. Ben, armed with the confidence that his record was now cleared and that

Robert would be providing a positive reference, had looked at the Times Educational Supplement website and applied for several primary teaching jobs in West Dorset. One, a village school in Symondsbury, just outside Bridport, had called him for interview and he was planning to drive down the week before the wedding.

On the day of the interview, he was just putting on his best suit in the morning, when his iPhone bleeped. Oh, nice, a text message from Lucy, maybe to wish him good luck. Had he told her about the interview? He couldn't remember.

"Can I call you?" said the text.

"That will be expensive, are you sure?" replied Ben.

"Sure I'm sure."

"Okay, but make it quick. I'll be driving soon."

Ben was eating a boiled egg prepared by his mother when the phone rang.

"Hi, Lucy, how are you?"

"I'm good. Are you sitting down?"

"Why? Have you got some sensational news?"

"You could say that. I'm eight weeks pregnant."

"Goodness! That's fantastic. Congratulations!"

"Is that all you have to say?"

"No, really, it's great. I'm really happy for you."

"Ben, I don't think you heard what I said. I said, I'm eight weeks pregnant."

Suddenly, the penny dropped.

"You mean… You mean…?"

"Yes, you're going to be a daddy."

"But how can you be sure?"

"I don't know what you think of me, but I'm not the type to sleep around, Ben. You're definitely the father."

"Christ!" The mixture of emotions was lethal. Joy, terror, fear, anticipation, confusion, guilt, exultation. Ben could hardly speak. "That's amazing!" was the best he could come up with. "Are you happy?"

"Sure I'm happy. Are you?"

"Yeah, of course I am. But what the hell am I going to do? I'm getting married next week."

"That's okay. You must do whatever you want. But promise to visit us sometimes."

Ben was picturing the beautiful Lucy, blossoming with child. At the same time, all his worries about the impending wedding and relocation, suppressed for months, came bubbling to the surface.

"Listen," he said, "I'm just off for a job interview. I have to go. But I'll ring you later and we'll talk."

Then he said it: "I love you."

Ben could hardly steer the car, far less understand the GPS lady. He negotiated the Dorchester bypass and the switchback coastal hills between there and Bridport. As he passed the road to the village of Eype, he realized he couldn't go through with it. He pulled into a lay-by and took out his mobile.

"Hello, is that Symondsbury Primary School?"

"Yes."

"My name is Mr Walker. I think I'm expected for interview this morning?"

"That's right."

"I'm afraid something has cropped up and I'm not going to be able to make it."

"Well, that's most inconvenient. Shall we reschedule the interview for later?"

"No, I'd like to withdraw my application."

Ben drove down the tiny lane to Eype's Mouth and drew into the car park overlooking the pebble beach and the massive grey waves crashing on to it. He took the little path to the right and struggled up the steep hill to the top of Thorncombe Beacon, a place he had often visited before when he needed to unclutter his head and think clearly. From here, he could see most of the Jurassic Coast and the infinite sea.

Ben knew this was the end of his adult life as he had known it. He'd reached a crossroads and suddenly, it was clear which way to go. Everything was going to change. He took his phone from his pocket, took a deep breath and dialled Lucy's number. Bugger, no signal. He had to drive half way to Abbotsbury before he got one bar on his phone.

"Lucy, I want to come and be with you. What do you say?"

"It's your decision, Ben, but if you want to come, I'm here. Oh, I mean me and a little someone else."

Suddenly, Ben felt calm. "I'll be with you soon."

"Whenever you're ready, I'll be waiting for you," replied Lucy.

Chapter 15

It was like the closing scene of an Agatha Christie novel. Ben had asked everyone to convene in the lounge at Chilbolton Avenue: Robert, Diana, Rosie and her sister Natalie, in town for bridesmaid rehearsals. He'd said he had something to tell them.

Ben had had a sleepless night mulling over how to break the news while causing the least damage. In the end, he texted Rosie to say he was coming up to Winchester and wanted to meet her in the flat in Taplings Road, as he had something he needed to say. As she let herself in, looking no more than mildly intrigued, he was waiting in the kitchen.

"This is all very mysterious," said Rosie, smiling. She clearly thought he'd had some clever idea to add a novel element to the wedding. "Don't say you're calling it off," she laughed.

Ben had had plenty of time to prepare his words, but he hadn't expected that question.

"Well, yes, actually."

Rosie's smile waned. "What do you mean?"

"I can't marry you."

There was a shocked pause. Rosie clearly still wasn't quite sure whether it was some kind of sick wind up.

"What you mean, you can't marry me? The wedding's in a couple of days, for goodness' sake."

"I know, but we're going to have to call it off."

"We can't call it off. Guests are coming from all over the country. Everything is booked. Besides, ..." – a more important thought entered her head - "why on earth do you want to call it off?"

"It's difficult to explain, Rosie. I've been thinking about it a lot and I'm just not ready. I don't want that life. I just don't fit in with your family and your friends."

There was quite a long silence as Rosie considered what he had said.

"I know what it is. It's that bloody pub. Are you going to tell me you've got off with one of those hippy girls from the canal?"

"No, no. Getting out of education and being with more unconventional people is part of it, but there's something else."

Rosie still hadn't got really angry, or even accepted what Ben was saying.

"Look, it's a frightening prospect for any man. You're worried about losing your freedom, I understand that. But you'll soon get used to it. Listen, there are lots of things going on in Dorset that you could get involved in, organic farming, music, ecological projects. They're all good things, you don't have to go back into teaching."

It was a well-meant olive branch, only making what Ben had to say even more difficult.

"I'm sorry, Rosie, but there's no easy way to tell you, so I'm just going to say it. I slept with Lucy Cruz and now she's pregnant."

He knew it was a bombshell, but Rosie's reaction was worse than he'd expected.

"You fucking what?" Rosie seldom swore, but now she found the ability. "You slept with that cow? I can't believe it. You fucking bastard, how could you? How could you? You pretend to love me and all the time, you're screwing that whore. Wait till Dad hears about this."

How typical that Dad needed to be brought into it straight away. It seemed that Ben could never escape from that man.

"I'm planning to tell him as soon as possible. I'm accepting responsibility for what happened. I'm very, very sorry, but I've given it a lot of thought and it's best for everyone if we split up."

"Best for you, you mean." It was like an unexpected bereavement, as all Rosie's long and short-term plans had turned to dust in the space of a few moments. No wonder she was furious. "You complete selfish bastard."

It was inevitable that crockery would fly. A mug narrowly missed Ben's head and smashed into the cooker hood. Why did I choose the kitchen, Ben asked itself? Any minute now, she's going to go for the cutlery drawer and we'll be looking at murder number two. But within a moment, Rosie slumped into a chair and laid her head on her hands on the kitchen table, tears of frustration, rage and incomprehension flowing onto her sleeves.

Ben was tempted to put his arm round her, but quickly decided that wouldn't be a good move in the circumstances. He waited until she had calmed down a bit and then told her what he planned to do.

"I'd like to meet up with your family later tonight, when you've had a chance to think about it, and then of course I'll go back to the Travelodge and leave you in peace."

Rosie looked up. Her smudged mascara and lank, dark hair made her look a bit like Alice Cooper, Ben noticed with discomfort.

"Isn't there some way we could work something out, make it all go away, and start again?"

"A baby isn't going to go away, Rosie. I didn't plan any of this, and I promise I only slept with her once, but I'm clear in my mind now. I have to be with Lucy and I have to be with my child, so I'll be going to Texas to see if I can start a new life there."

Later, in the house in Chilbolton Avenue, Ben had prepared a little speech. He was pretty sure Rosie would already have told the family, and he was right. As he entered the room, both Rosie and Natalie were red-eyed from crying, while the more controlled adults were clearly steaming with self-righteous rage. Ben had known what Diana's priorities would be, and he was right.

"We'll have to cancel everything, the ceremony, the reception, the hotel for all the people we've invited." Ben hardly knew any of the people, but had reluctantly come to accept that the entire event was being staged for the benefit of others. "What will people say?"

"I know it's embarrassing for you, but..."

"It's more than embarrassing, it's devastating. After all we've done for you."

Ben didn't really think they'd actually done much for him at all, considering the wedding had been so much a case of "keeping up appearances". But he kept quiet.

Now it was Robert's turn. He'd been waiting, building up to the inevitable outburst.

"You needn't think you're going to get a reference for me, ever."

"I don't want a reference."

Robert ignored him. "And you can expect to be invoiced for all the expense we have gone to. There's the deposit for Lainston House. There's all the champagne, that's non-refundable. My cousins are flying in from Australia, they'll have to cancel their flights. What about the limo we booked?" The list went on and on.

That reminded Diana of something. "We've even booked a surprise honeymoon for you in the Maldives. What will happen with that?"

"Maybe you two could go. That's very kind of you, by the way, I'm really sorry."

"We'll bloody need a holiday after this fiasco," said Robert, then, almost as an afterthought: "I ought to give you a damn good thrashing. It's no more than you deserve." He almost looked as if he might do it, taking one menacing step towards Ben, before thinking better of it.

There was silence, apart from the sobs of Rosie and Natalie. Rosie had had her say and Natalie was so shocked that she had nothing to contribute.

Ben tried to be more pragmatic. "We need to take some practical steps right away. There are lots of people we need to inform..."

"Whatever will the vicar say?" wailed Diana.

"I'm more than happy to help in any way I can," offered Ben.

"Help? Help?" Robert was shouting now. "We'll take no help from you, young man. Get out of our house and don't come back. We never want to see you again." He advanced towards Ben, grabbed him brusquely by the arm, guided him to the front door, opened it and pushed him out. Ben stumbled on the gravel, before raising his hands in a gesture of surrender.

"Okay, if that's what you want. I'm truly sorry..."

"We don't want your apology, you hypocritical bastard. Get out of my sight."

The door slammed and Ben found himself wandering down Romsey Road in a daze. In the short term, all he could do was once again get on the phone to the Travelodge. In the longer term, it would have to be back to his parents in Chew Magna for a while. One thing was for sure, the meeting he had just had was proof that he had made the right decision.

....

Expensive phone calls to America became the norm in the next few weeks, as Ben prepared to head to Austin. His parents, initially surprised, to say the least, had accepted that his move was a good one. He handed in his notice at The Narrowboat, reluctantly accepted by Phil Clark, and double-checked the validity of his ESTA entry permit for the USA, something which made everything seem more official. He had to put contact details of where he'd be staying, so entered Lucy's address in the online application form. "Bloody hell," he thought, "this is really happening."

And really happening it was. A fortnight after he should have married

Rosie (he could have been on a beach in the Maldives, Ben realized, pretty much his only regret about the entire sequence of events), he was on a flight to Atlanta, from where he would connect on to Austin. He'd left virtually all his possessions in Taplings Road. All he needed initially was a few clothes and if bridges were burnt, so be it.

This time, the embrace between Lucy and Ben at Austin's Bergstrom airport was much less tentative. Somehow, a bond had grown between the two of them, a bond that had become a lot stronger through Lucy's pregnancy. Ben couldn't believe how things had turned out. The beautiful Lucy had chosen him above all the musclebound Texans she could have had. How was this possible? "It's your lovely English accident," laughed Lucy, whenever he would ask.

Lucy showed Ben the news item she had cut out from the Austin American Statesman about the outcome of the trial:

> *"A man has been convicted and sentenced to life imprisonment for the murder of Austin music legend Corey Zander. The ex-leader of the Oklahoma country rock band The Grams had just played his first ever concert in the UK when he was killed in what appears to have been a chance attack after clashing with a drunk man in a pub in England's ancient capital, Winchester. This represents the final episode in the life of a musician who colleagues claimed to be "cursed", on account of the many misfortunes in his life. A tribute concert to Zander was held at SXSW in March, raising money for his educational charity, the Corey Zander Foundation. Zander leaves a daughter, Lucy Cruz, a respected South Austin artist."*

Ben moved straight into the little house on South Congress with Lucy. There were appointments with the midwife to arrange, many new friends to meet, as well as looking into the practicalities of how he could stay in America long term. The tourist visa allowed him to stay for six months, so a temporary job was an early priority to sort out. Enquiries showed that an eventual attaining of a Green Card was possible, but would be difficult and complicated. Briefly, they wondered about a marriage of convenience, but quickly decided that would be premature. "I hardly know you," smiled Lucy.

A job sorted itself out sooner than expected. On Ben's first Thursday in Austin, Lucy wanted to show him an institution of the city, the weekly free live show by Ian Mclagan and the Bump Band. Only in Austin could you go and see a music legend for free in a pub, but Mclagan had a special relationship with the city. Originally in the Small Faces, then the Faces and the Rolling Stones, the tiny, white-haired Hammond organist had emigrated to America, ending up in Austin in 1994, where he now was a musical eminence. And every Thursday, he and his band played in a downtown bar called the Lucky Lounge.

Lucy seemed to know every musician in town, and it wasn't long before Ben found himself chatting with Jon Notharthomas, the Bump Band's affable bassist. Extraordinarily, it transpired that Notharthomas owned a small chain of hot dog stands going by the groan-worthy name of Best Wurst. Before he knew what was happening, Ben found himself agreeing to man one of the stands, just near Buffalo Billiards on Sixth Street, from where, for the next few weeks, he dispensed Chilli Dogs to the passing throngs of students every evening until 2 am. It was a fabulous job, because of the good-natured, laid-back friendliness of the people, such a contrast to the tense aggression to be found on UK streets late at night.

During the day, Ben helped Lucy out with her various projects. She was preparing for an exhibition of her work to be held in Denton, so there was plenty to do in the way of transporting canvases, handing out flyers and suchlike. Lucy also told Ben about her current pet project, a tribute CD of Corey Zander songs, to be recorded by Austin musical luminaries and sold in aid of the Corey Zander Foundation. Ben said he would gladly take on this task, and set to work to recruit people. Ramona Cullis kindly let him have the use of a room in the Yard Dog Gallery as an office.

Many of the people who'd performed at the gig at the Continental signed up straight away. Alejandro Escovedo's backing band, the Sensitive Boys, agreed to provide any backing tracks needed. To ensure good sales, Ben needed to approach bigger stars as well, so had to deal with some record companies and managers. The goodwill was there but some of the bigger artists, such as Willie Nelson and Hayes Carll, were hard to get hold of. Eventually, after several months, Ben had got a tentative track listing together. Some artists simply recorded their contributions in their home studios, others needed financing for studio time, but this seemed to be a worthwhile investment of Foundation money, which would eventually bring in revenue. It was hard work and all completely new to Ben, but he loved it because everything about the project was so positive, in stark contrast to recent events in his life.

It was only now that Ben realized that he'd never really been happy in adult life. Those first few initial years of teaching had been filled with stress and bureaucracy. Then there were the irritating kids, many of them over-protected and spoilt. Pushy parents would complain about absolutely anything, and sometimes the responsibility was overwhelming.

On top of that had come the engagement to Rosie. Looking back, he knew that he'd given in to pressure. He was too inexperienced in life to be settling down so early, but he had seemed caught up in a flowing tide of conventionality, against which he seemed powerless to battle. Most of his old friends from university had "settled down" in safe jobs and stable, unadventurous relationships, and that just seemed the way things had to be.

In a crazy way, he was grateful to Corey Zander for shaking his life up. At least the last six months couldn't have been accused of being boring. But he'd spent most of the time feeling frightened, unappreciated and under extreme strain. He became aware that here, in the Austin sunshine, he was waking up without a headache for the first time in years.

Much of this was down to Lucy. She simply took everything in her stride.

As the bump grew, she blossomed as well but made no attempt to reduce her level of creative activity, picking away at her guitar whenever she wasn't painting or arranging a show. Plus, the two of them made time to walk, hand-in-hand, through Austin's parks, watching the parents with small children they would soon be joining

The tribute CD was finally ready to go. The mixture of tracks was intriguing. An ancient, punky Chocs song called "Ready For Fun" was given a cheery western swing makeover by an Austin quartet called the Jitterbug Vipers. The virtuoso Texan guitarist Monte Montgomery did an atmospheric rearrangement of the Grams' signature tune "Desert Grave", while some more recent Corey Zander solo songs were covered by Bob Schneider and Sam Baker. "Mad And Bad" was eventually allocated to Bob Cheevers. By the time he'd finished with it, it had been turned from a rock anthem into a reflective, pedal steel guitar led country ballad, but worked just as well. The idea had been for a low-key local launch, but by the time the record was complete, the quality and the line-up were so impressive that Ben was emboldened to try for a major release. He approached a number of labels and eventually settled on Bloodshot, home of Jon Langford (another UK expat who had chosen Chicago as his place to settle). This Chicago label was strong in the alternative rock field and also had connections with the Yard Dog Gallery, so the choice was perfect. Plus they had worldwide distribution. In that ghoulish and deeply ironic way that characterizes an artist who dies in unusual or tragic circumstances, interest in Corey Zander was far greater after his death than it had ever been when he was alive.

As Ben was gainfully employed in Austin, he was able, with the help of a few influential friends, to gain sponsorship for a working visa, which made him safe and legal for the foreseeable future. Christmas approached and with it, the prospect of Lucy giving birth. The baby was due in mid-December and Lucy was determined that it should all be completely natural. She'd been continuing her healthy and active lifestyle and hoped for a home birth. As it turned out, the contractions began late on December

23 and the midwife noticed a couple of things which made her decide to recommend a transfer to hospital. Ben and Lucy agreed that safety was paramount and the little girl was eventually delivered on Christmas Eve in Austin's St David's Hospital.

Lucy was exhausted and beautiful; Ben was ecstatic. How things had changed in less than a year, and how brilliant everything was. There was much discussion about what to call the baby, with Christmassy names like Holly and Eve being bandied around, but eventually, Ben's desire for a proper rock 'n' roll name was satisfied. He was after something along the lines of Justin Townes Earle, so they ended up with Alexandra Walker-Cruz. That way, if she grew up to be a singer, there'd be no need to invent a stage name.

The love Ben felt for his daughter knew no bounds. The feeling of closeness as he strolled the pathways of Zilker Park with little Alexandra strapped to his chest in a sling was like nothing he had ever experienced. Lucy was a perfect mother, conscientiously and successfully breastfeeding her daughter.

The album, with cover artwork by Lucy and liner notes by Allan Jones, was eventually launched in March, just a year after the tribute concert. The venue was Waterloo Records and a good crowd heard an acoustic set by Will Johnson and a duet between Lucy and Ben (on harmony vocals) on an obscure Chocs demo they'd found on an old cassette. It was a song about Corey's ancestors' heritage and it was entitled "Tears Of Dust". Ben was terrified and paralysed by stage fright, especially as some of the audience had tears in their eyes. He was in even more of a state when the time came to him to make a speech, something that Lucy had coerced him into doing.

"It's hard to believe where I am now, not much more than a year since I was a boring schoolteacher in a boring English town." He gestured towards Alexandra, sleeping peacefully in her buggy alongside the shelves of vinyl. "It's a dreadful irony that the person I have to thank for this is Lucy's father, Corey Zander." There was a ripple of applause.

"Corey died in terrible circumstances. We all know about them, so I won't dwell on it. But every day of my life, I think about the fact that, if I hadn't booked Corey to play on that day, he might still be alive today. So Lucy and I wanted to prove that out of bad can come good. Wonderful, generous people have contributed to this great album and all profits from it will go to the Corey Zander Foundation, helping to educate the children of impoverished musicians, of whom there are plenty in Austin." A rueful laugh of recognition went round the shop.

An iced Margarita machine had been brought in for the occasion, so Ben asked everyone present to raise their glasses. "It's important not to look back. Corey would have wanted us all to have fun today and that's what we're going to do." Glasses clinked as people lined up at the till to buy the CD. Weeks of discussion hadn't been able to produce a title that everyone agreed on, so it was simply called "Corey Zander: A Tribute."

....

For the first couple of years of young Alexandra's life (they couldn't bring themselves to call her Alex, so settled on Ali), Ben worked full-time running the Foundation on his own, distributing funds to those in need and organizing "exciting" events like Easter Egg Hunts and picnics. He was able to put himself on a small salary, and Lucy's career was going well too. Her creative work was able to fit snugly alongside looking after Ali, and the family moved to a small, clapperboard house with a garden in the southern suburbs.

When Ali was three, they rented a Slipstream camper van and toured America for six months, something they felt they had to do before she reached school age. They couldn't resist visiting some of the places that Corey had been to in his career, like San Francisco and Los Angeles. After some discussion, they decided also to visit Tahlequah to see where his roots had really lain. Sir Lance-A-Lot was boarded up, a victim of competition from chains like Wendy's and Taco Bell. Lucy had stayed in touch with the members of The Grams and they visited Jesse, who'd arranged for

Mark and Will to come round with their wives, children and – yes – their grandchildren, for a barbecue in the garden. From those guys, they were able to glean instructions for how to find the woods where Corey had grown up.

They parked on the edge of the woods near Wagoner, now designated as a protected area. The trailer had, of course, long since collapsed and been removed. As the weak sunshine glinted between the leaves, making dappled patterns on the ground, they pictured young Alexander toddling around, just as his granddaughter and namesake was obliviously doing now. It was a bitter-sweet experience, and one which was to have unexpected consequences.

Back in Austin, months later, Lucy was messing about with Corey's old acoustic guitar and came up with a little chorus, based on their visit to his woodland home:

> *"In the deep dark woods where you came from,*
> *We can feel your presence like you've never been gone."*

She worried that it might seem over-sentimental or maudlin, but ploughed on with the writing until the song was complete, finally doing a rough recording on her home computer. Ben, at work in the office, knew nothing of this until a few days later, when Lucy plucked up courage to play it to him, a solo performance in the kitchen, with young Ali on tambourine. As the last chord died away, Ben gasped.

"Bloody hell." His anglicisms hadn't been fully knocked out of him yet. "That's incredible. I think it's a hit!" he laughed, doing his best Simon Cowell impersonation.

Ben's immediate instinct was to issue the song as a single in aid of the Foundation. Sales of the album had long since peaked and dwindled, and there was a limit to the number of tribute concerts that could be organized. After the Continental Club extravaganza, anything else couldn't help but be an anti-climax. But Bloodshot Records, to whom he sent the demo, were immediately interested, asking whether there were any more where that one came from. Of course, there were. Over the years, Lucy had accumulated more than a dozen original songs, never intending them to be for public consumption beyond small open mic nights at bars in Texas.

It was a good moment to launch a career for Lucy. Childcare could be arranged for Ali, and Ben was able to reduce his hours at the Foundation to help out with "managing" her. The record company put no undue pressure on her but did come up with a small advance to help finance the recording. Now fully immersed in Austin's artistic and musical scene, Ben was able to put together a dream band to record the ten songs which were eventually selected: on bass and drums, Bobby Daniel and Chris Searles from the Sensitive Boys, and on guitar, "Scrappy" Judd Newcomb from the Bump Band. Between them, they pushed Lucy to have the courage to project her sweet voice with more confidence than she had ever summoned up before. The whole thing was recorded live in Lucy and Ben's front room. Even with the blinds drawn, you could still, if you listened intently, hear the birds singing in the trees outside. The album was christened "Lucy Cruz: In The Deep Dark Woods".

From the record company's point of view, it was a dream project. The master tapes were delivered to them complete and ready to press. The songs were highly emotional, not crassly commercial, but accessible and radio-friendly nonetheless. There was an obvious "angle" to be pursued, with Corey's legend again being used as a hook. Investing in a good PR company paid off, as first internet radio came on board, followed by the music press (Filter magazine selected it as Album Of The Month), then country and rock radio nationwide, then the general press and eventually television. For Ben, the biggest thrill was looking at the tiny print on the CD insert: Tambourine: Ali Walker-Cruz; Backing vocals and Executive Producer: Ben Walker.

When the call came for a performance of "In The Deep Dark Woods" on the David Letterman show, one of the important angles was that Lucy had stated that she wouldn't be touring. Unlike artists like Alanis Morissette, who opted to take their infants on the tour bus with them, Lucy strongly felt that a quiet and stable upbringing was what was required for Ali. But it didn't particularly matter. Once the nation had heard the song on coast-to-coast TV, the sales momentum took on a life of its own and the song became a chart hit, ironically getting higher than any of her father's records ever had.

It was five years after Corey's death when Ben, Lucy and Ali headed back to the UK for the first time. With support from "Q" and "Mojo" magazines, Lucy's profile in the UK had grown to the extent where she had been offered a solo slot on "Later With Jools Holland." She performed the single live, with Jools insisting on adding not very appropriate boogie piano, and the next day they took the train down to Bradford-on-Avon.

Ben had made Phil Clark promise not to make a big deal about their secret appearance at the Narrowboat, so the only way anyone knew about it was from a small handwritten sign which was put in the window a couple of hours before the show. Word that that girl who'd been on TV the night before would be performing in their local pub spread like wildfire through the small town, and the place was packed as Lucy performed a brief six-song set and Ben passed a hat round for donations in aid of the Kennet and Avon Canal Restoration Society.

The hatchet had long since been buried between Ben and Rosie. When Ali was born, Ben had taken the risk of sending a card to her. He didn't know what the reaction would be, but there was nothing to be lost. In fact, she explained in her reply, it had only been a couple of months before David Watson, one of her colleagues at Poole's, had plucked up courage to ask her out, eventually declaring that he had fancied her for years from the next-door desk. Rosie and David had married a year later, with the reception, of course, at Lainston House, so the champagne got used after all. Rosie and Ben came to the civilized conclusion that, as their lives had both moved on, there was nothing to be gained from blanking each other. Rosie now also had a toddler, Jack, but as the children played together in the garden of the Black Boy, Rosie explained that Robert wouldn't be willing to meet them. He would never get over what he saw as the ultimate betrayal, and would never speak to Ben again.

"How are things at school?" asked Ben.

"He's not there any more. I've been waiting to tell you in person. It's bad news, I'm afraid. He's had to take early retirement."

"Blimey," said Ben, "gross misconduct? What's he been up to? Molesting the school secretary?"

It was an inappropriate piece of attempted levity, as Ben was soon to find out.

"Actually, it's serious. He's been diagnosed with cancer."

Ben blushed, embarrassed at his lack of sensitivity. "Shit, I'm so sorry," he said. No matter how fractious their relationship had been, he didn't wish anything like that on Robert.

"Yes, it's a particularly virulent form of pancreatic cancer, I'm afraid. He's having chemo and Mum is looking after him, but the doctors are clear that it's only a matter of months."

Chapter 16

It was six weeks later that Ben took the call at home in Austin. After the storm of activity surrounding Lucy's career breakthrough, things had quietened down. Lucy was unwilling to take part in the album / tour / album pattern that conventional music business wisdom required. Taking Kate Bush as a model, and with Ben's full support, she was going to put her private life first and her career second.

"It's happened," Rosie was saying.

"You mean Robert?"

"Yes, he passed away yesterday."

She had rung to ask if Ben wanted to come to the funeral. After some thought, he decided he would. Life was too short to hold grudges, and in a way, Robert had been important in his life. Ali had started school and Lucy, having never met Robert, decided to stay home with her.

It was an odd feeling to be back at Basingstoke Crematorium. This time, the crowd of mourners was much bigger. There were colleagues, past and present, representatives from the County Council Education Department and the Rotary Club plus relatives and friends from far and wide. Fulsome tributes were paid to Robert for his years of dedicated service to the young people of Winchester. Everyone was dressed in sombre black and a feeling of extreme sadness filled the chapel. Classical music was played as the coffin disappeared, and then everyone repaired to the Winchester Lawn Tennis Club in Bereweeke Road for drinks and sandwiches. Ben decided not to go along. He felt he had done his bit, and a distraught Diana was steadfast in not speaking to him or even casting him a glance. Ben certainly didn't want to cause further grief or embarrassment.

As Ben walked to his hire car, he paused to shake Rosie's hand and kiss her on the cheek. She was with her husband David and son Jack. Rosie fumbled in her handbag and took out a brown A5 envelope.

"We were cleaning out Dad's desk yesterday and we came across this. It's addressed to you."

"Really? That's interesting, thanks. I'll have a look later." Ben put the letter into the inside pocket of his suit. He wasn't sure where to go or what to do, and in the end he decided to go for a cappuccino in a nearby coffee shop called The Good Life in Kings Worthy. This was a favourite old haunt from his days at St John's School, where he would often take a pile of exercise books for marking. After he had ordered, he took out the envelope. It was clearly marked, in Robert's handwriting: "For the sole attention of Ben Walker. Only to be opened in the event of my death."

Inside was a sheaf of folded A4 papers, typed on a computer and printed out. Ben, hoping that it would be a protracted apology for the way he had been treated, began to read.

Dear Ben,

By the time you read this, I will no longer be with you. My specialist has recently informed me that I only have a few weeks to live. Before I die, there is something important I have to tell you. Barry Mort did not kill Corey Zander. It was me.

I know this will come as a shock to you. I am writing this letter to explain exactly what happened and to ask for your understanding and forgiveness. There are many things that you do not know and could not have known.

On the evening when you went to Millbrook to buy drugs for Corey, Rosie was left alone in the house. I am afraid that things happened that evening that you now need to know about, even though we decided to keep them from you at the time. Corey Zander was talking to Rosie in the lounge and she gave him a couple of glasses of the whiskey you had bought, to be hospitable. All this is what Rosie told me, so I know it to be accurate. Alone in the house with her, Zander started making suggestive remarks to Rosie. He said she was attractive and asked if he could touch her. She, of course, laughed and said no, but he didn't want to take no for an answer. He was a very big man, and he pinned her down on the sofa. He put his hand on her breast and, while she struggled, he then put his other hand up her skirt and tried to pull down her pants. All the time, she said, he was laughing and saying that she wanted it really. Of course, she didn't want it. In the end, she got her hand on one of her mother's crochet needles and managed to stab him in the arm with it. As he pulled back in pain, Rosie succeeded in escaping from underneath him and ran for the door. She went home to your flat. We were out, of course, looking after Diana's mother, and didn't return until the next day.

I didn't want to come to your gig at all, but Rosie wanted me to show support. While you were helping to set up, Rosie asked me to come into the beer garden, and that was where she told me what had happened. I was absolutely incensed. I understand that you have a daughter now as well, so you will know how a father feels if anyone threatens or harms his daughter. You would do anything to protect her. She had been molested in my own house and I hadn't been there to help.

My instinct was to go straight to Zander and confront him, but there were too many people around. In my position, I couldn't afford any scandal, and a brawl in a pub could have meant the end of my career. Then, before I knew it, all that trouble was kicking off. Barry Mort barged in to watch the student band and then he caused even worse trouble when Zander was playing. For a moment, I thought Zander was going to kill him, but then Zander suddenly left the room.

That was my chance to get away. I promise that all I intended to do was make sure I wasn't involved in any potential fallout.

I was just leaving when I saw the glow of a cigarette at the end of the car park. I was sure it was Zander, and I was right. I went up to him and confronted him with what he had done to my daughter. It would never have ended the way it did if he had responded in the right way and apologized, but he didn't. He was still wound up by what Mort had said to him, and he didn't need my accusations as well. He just swore at me. What did it was the words he used: "She was asking for it."

I did not intend to kill him. Please don't think I came up behind him and attacked him with a brick. But what the barristers were saying was partly right. I was beside myself with rage and I pushed him as hard as I could. I would never have had the strength to push him over, but he put his foot on a slippery old kebab paper and just went down backwards like a log. I was horrified when I saw he'd hit his head, with all that blood coming out. I had no idea whether he was dead or not, but I didn't care. The only important thing was that I couldn't be associated in any way with such sordid events. I dragged him behind the dustbin. It wasn't far but it was difficult. He was very heavy, I can tell you. Then I put the brick and the Bourbon bottle in the bin.

I crept back towards the road, keeping in the shadows. Suddenly, Mort came dashing out. He called to his friends to get away fast, and they ran off. That's when I realized that no one knew that I had spoken to Zander, or even where he was. As I began to walk home, I suddenly saw that there was blood all over my suit and my hands. I obviously couldn't go home like that, so I took the back streets to school. I let myself in with the master key. I sometimes have to go in to do jobs in the evening, so I know how to override the alarm system. I keep a spare suit and shirt in the cupboard in the office in case I get paint or something on my clothes. I buried the bloodstained suit at the bottom of the skip at the back of the school. I knew nobody would dream of looking in it. Why should they?

Then I went home. In the morning, I told Diana that there had been trouble at the gig and that it had over-run. I didn't know whether Zander was dead. For all I knew, he'd woken up and was walking around with a sore head. It wasn't until the next evening that I was sure I'd killed him, and by then they had arrested you.

Ben, please believe me when I say that, if the police had pursued the case against you, I would have gone in and confessed. I wouldn't have let you go down for a crime you hadn't committed. But when they saw that Mort was the obvious killer, I realized I had a chance to make sure that both you and I would be safe. Mort was a vile, violent man with no scruples or morals. He might easily have killed Zander. I remembered reading a report of a previous attempted murder he had been involved in. The world would be a better place with people like that safely locked up behind bars.

The only problem was, was there enough evidence to convict him? That's when I realized that I could provide evidence. If I said I had seen Zander and Mort arguing and fighting, it should be enough to convince a jury. That way, both you and I would be able to continue our careers with our reputations intact.

Please don't blame Rosie for not telling you about what Zander did to her. She hadn't had a chance to talk to you, and planned to tell you all about it the next day. I begged her not to, because you would have told the police about it. That would have made me a suspect and I couldn't afford that. As far as I know, she still hasn't told you. Her motives were good; she was only trying to protect her father.

Now a final request. For the sake of everyone, I beg you to burn this letter and never to tell Diana or Rosie about it. I know you will grant me this final wish, as you wouldn't want to hurt them either. It would kill them. I want them still to be proud of me as a husband and father. I made a terrible mistake, but it doesn't make me a bad person.

Yours affectionately,

Robert

Ben looked around at all the middle-class mums enjoying a coffee and chat. None of them could possibly suspect that the pale-faced man in the corner had just read a confession to manslaughter. Ben felt sick. His head was spinning. His immediate thought was, no, Mr Leighton, you are indeed a bad person, a very bad person. Your selfishness knows no bounds. For the sake of your reputation you were willing to let an innocent person be locked up, missing his child's early years. You lied under oath and now you want me to allow Mort to continue to languish in prison, just to protect the sensibilities of your family. Well, you chose the wrong person.

The first thing to decide was whether to tell the family or the police first. For a moment, he was about to stride into the wake at the tennis club and wave the letter at the assembled dignitaries, but in the end, he drove straight to North Walls police station. DCI Bird had been transferred to another post in Fareham, but Jackson had been promoted and taken his place. He didn't even know that Robert had died, and read the letter in dumbfounded amazement. Tomorrow, he would have to consult his superiors about the procedure for initiating a pardon, something he'd never had to deal with before.

Ben was staggered that the letter contained not a jot of empathy for the falsely-imprisoned Mort. So self-obsessed had Robert been, so scornful of what he saw as the criminal classes, that he hadn't given him a thought. He wanted to protect his family? Well, tough, because his family deserved to know just what kind of man he had been. The wake was due to end at six, so at seven, Ben was ringing the doorbell at Chilbolton Avenue. Diana was in, and so were Rosie and her husband.

When Diana opened the door, she tried to slam it back in Ben's face when she saw who the visitor was, but Ben got his foot in place, preventing the door from shutting.

"You needn't think you can take advantage of my grief to make me forgive you," she shouted. "We said we never wanted to see you again, and we meant it."

"I'm not the one who needs forgiving, Diana," said Ben, quietly. Through the gap in the door, he passed her one of the photocopies that Jackson had made of Robert's letter. "Read this."

"Why should I? What is it?"

"Just read it. If you don't want me to come in, that's okay."

The door closed and Ben sat down on a garden bench. His life, so calm and contented for years, had once again gone weird. But at least he now felt in control. He had something important to do. In his pocket was the second photocopy of the letter. Ben stood up and walked towards Romsey Road, up to the top of Stanmore Lane, then turned left down the hill and into Thurmond Road. Would Shelley still be living in the house where Mort used to live? It was unlikely, but possible. He knocked on the door of the house he thought might be theirs, but it was answered by a big man in a stained vest.

"Yeah?"

"I wonder if a lady called Shelley lives here?"

"She does. What do you want?"

A small boy poked his head round the man's legs.

"Is this Shelley's son?"

"Yeah, who wants to know?"

"I've got something for Shelley."

"Who's that, Darren?" came a woman's voice from inside the house.

"Someone for you."

Shelley appeared, looking anxious. "Can I help you? ... Bloody hell, I know who you are."

Ben decided to do away with any niceties.

"Yes, I'm Ben Walker. I'm here to tell you that Barry is innocent. He's been innocent all along."

"What?" The colour had drained from her face.

"Read this. It will explain everything."

"You'd better come in."

Ben stood with the big man, either a lover or a relative, he assumed, while Shelley sat on the sofa and read the letter. When she finished, she looked up.

"Is this some kind of wind-up?"

"No, Shelley, it's the truth at last."

"I knew it. I bloody knew he never done it."

"I told the police, so he'll be out soon. Until this afternoon, I had no idea of any of this. He didn't tell anyone. I don't even know why he told me. Somewhere in there, he must have had a conscience. Anyway, it's over."

Now Ben had a decision to make. Should he attempt to talk to Diana and Rosie or should he just go back to Texas and try to carry on with his life? In the end, he did pluck up courage to go back to Chilbolton Avenue and ring the doorbell again. Both women were in tears and poor David was hopelessly trying to comfort them. But nothing he, Ben or anyone else could have said would have helped. Their lives had collapsed.

"How could you?" Diana's voice was rasping and cracked. "He asked you to burn it. Couldn't you have obeyed his last wish and spared us this torment?"

"No, I couldn't."

"Please God you haven't shown it to anyone else?"

"I took it straight to the police."

"But the man is dead. What good can that do now?"

"What good? What good? Have you learned nothing? Do you want Mort to rot in jail for something he didn't do?"

"But what about us?"

This was too much. "I don't care about you. I care about what's right."

Ben had nothing more to say. His flight back to sanity was the next morning.

Chapter 17

Barry Mort was released from prison within days. Ben didn't know for sure what became of him. Maybe Shelley had started a new relationship, possibly with the bloke who answered the door, and Mort now had no home to go to. Perhaps he hooked up with his old "gang" and they looked after him. Possibly he stormed into the house in Thurmond Road and confronted the new lover. Maybe he attacked him and ended up back in prison. Or it was possible that he was, indeed, a reformed character. Shelley might have taken him back and he'd turned into a responsible family man. Stranger things have happened. But anyway, Ben never found out and didn't really care. His life had moved on and he wasn't interested in looking backwards. Through emails from ex-colleagues, though, he did find out what became of the Leightons. The shame, and possible fear of reprisals, meant that they couldn't possibly stay in Winchester. Diana sold the house in Chilbolton Avenue at a good profit and moved to a small flat in Eastbourne, where she was able to establish a social life playing bridge and doing charity work, her reputation unsullied by a past that nobody knew about. The house was demolished and the spacious gardens were used to construct a block of luxury apartments overlooking the golf course. Diana held on to the student houses, which generated a generous monthly income for her.

Rosie and David also had to get away. The small-town gossip and finger-pointing soon became unbearable. Within a year, they had gone into partnership in a successful property business near Dijon, in France. They had two more children and, like Diana, were able to lead a relatively normal life. Of course, a dark cloud hung over it, but they were the only ones who knew.

In America, Ben had a family, a home and a job. But it wasn't without its challenges. Corey's posthumous record sales had dwindled to almost nothing. The Foundation had come to the end of its natural life and the Yard Dog could no longer spare the office space. On re-entering the USA, he'd been subjected to some awkward questioning by the border authorities. He was able to live as a "kept man" on Lucy's continuing royalties, and did his best to help run her career, but, to the frustration of the record company, she wasn't interested in recording a follow-up album. Ben could have become a chauffeur for her, just as she had been for her dad, but a life of gigging wasn't compatible with bringing up their daughter. Lucy's success had come by pure chance, but it wasn't a career she had ever aspired to. She wanted to stay at home, to be a mother, and to paint.

Until then, the life and love of Ben and Lucy had been unrealistically idyllic. Now, Robert's confession presented them with the greatest challenge they would ever face. Realistically, the best way to guarantee resident status for Ben would be for him and Lucy to get married, but when he broached the subject, it led to the first and last argument the two of them would ever have.

"The last time you were planning to marry someone, her father ended up killing my dad. Do you think that showed good judgement by you?"

"Don't be ridiculous. You can't blame Rosie for the actions of her dad. If we're going to go down that route, let me remind you that the reason he killed Corey was because your father attempted to rape my fiancée. Do you think that's fair?"

These were cruel and bitter words that arguably would have been better not being aired. But confronting the issue, far from driving them apart, allowed them to re-assess their love. They suddenly became aware that little Ali was looking on and listening, wide-eyed, to the unaccustomed raised voices. Ben's eyes met Lucy's and in that moment, they knew they would be together for ever.

"Dammit, it's the Curse of Zander causing trouble again!"

There was a twinkle in Ben's eyes as he said the ridiculous words. How would Lucy respond?

"Ungrateful bastard, after all we've done for him!"

The two of them laughed, embraced and brought little Ali into a family hug. They weren't responsible for their families' failings and together, they would forge a new and stronger life for themselves. Within months, their wedding had taken place, a quiet event which was carried out, for a laugh, in a tacky chapel in Las Vegas, complete with Ali as bridesmaid and an Elvis impersonator carrying out the ceremony.

Back in Austin, Ben, now armed with his Green Card, started a postgraduate course at the University of Texas that would qualify him to teach English to Hispanic immigrants seeking to improve their language skills. He was a natural teacher, and working with adults was far more intellectually rewarding than coping with the spoilt brats of Winchester.

One more matter had to be confronted. Ben's parents had become increasingly old and frail, and as their only son, there were responsibilities that Ben had to shoulder. His father had been diagnosed with Parkinson's Disease and he and Ben's mother were both living in a care home in Sidmouth, on the Devon coast. They had been forced to sell the family home in Chew Magna, and the exorbitant care home fees had already eaten up almost all the revenue from the house sale. In the end, word came from his mother that his father had passed away. Coming to terms with this awful news, he asked Lucy and Ali to accompany him once more to carry out a sad duty in the UK.

Sidmouth in May sounded quite appealing, but the reality was less so. While Lucy and Ali spent a few days in London, Ben helped his mother to arrange the funeral and work through all the bureaucracy of probate. She was very unwell herself, exhausted from dealing with her husband's illness and traumatized by her loss, and in the end, she didn't survive her husband by many months.

Ben had the idea of taking Ali to show her Bradford-on-Avon, but it turned out to be an unrewarding visit, and one which reinforced the wisdom of committing himself to a life in the USA. He hadn't received any replies to his emails to Phil Clark for months, and the explanation, as they got off the train, was plain to see. The Narrowboat was boarded up, adorned with a planning application to turn it into apartments. Of his old friends there was no sign. The canal restoration project had long since been completed and they had all moved on.

Before they returned to Texas, Ben had one more thing he wanted to show his family. He would always remember the place where he'd made the fateful decision to cancel his wedding to Rosie, withdraw his job application and commit himself to Lucy. He wanted Lucy and Ali to experience the Dorset area's legendary artistic heritage: the novels of Thomas Hardy, the music of Robert Fripp and PJ Harvey. He told them about the myth that, if you were lucky, you might bump into Harvey in the Hope and Anchor, or one of the other quaint Bridport pubs. It didn't happen, of course, but one morning, they had a vegetarian breakfast in the famous Hive Café on Burton Bradstock beach and took a secret peek at Billy Bragg's house nearby.

On the last afternoon, Ben drove the hire car down the tiny lane to the Anchor Inn at Seatown. He wanted the family to experience the glory of the cliffs at Thorncombe Beacon, with its incredible views over Lyme Bay to the west and Chesil Beach to the east. It was a long, hard climb and Lucy, now pregnant with their second child, puffed to the top and sat for a moment on the bench by the beacon to regain her breath. The infinite ocean stretched away to the horizon as the waves crashed onto the shingle beach below. In a strange way, it reminded them both of the joyful day at the Oasis at Lake Travis, where Lucy and Ben's relationship had been so new and thrilling. Now, it had developed into something much stronger, their shared experiences binding the family together.

Standing with her loved ones in this magical spot, the inspiration over the years for so much poetry, art and music, Lucy felt, for the first time in years, a song beginning to stir in her heart. Maybe, just maybe, a follow-up to "In The Deep Dark Woods" would finally be recorded.

"Waves washing over my life
Come and wash over me."

The words popped, fully formed, into her mind. The Curse Of Zander had finally been washed away.

END

Also by Oliver Gray:

VOLUME
A cautionary tale of rock and roll obsession

V.A.C.A.T.I.O.N.
Cautionary tales of travelling without style

ALAB (with Eddie Hardin)
35 years of musical mayhem on the road with the Spencer Davis Group

ACCESS ONE STEP
The official history of the Joiner's Arms

All published by Sarsen Press, Winchester, UK